PRAISE

"A collection of brief, delightful departures—and a few welcome chills. A truly enjoyable and impressive anthology."

—Tosca Lee, New York Times Bestselling author

"This collection presents a satisfying spectrum of storytellers, some familiar and others new on the scene. Some of the tales are unsettling and some are comforting; many are thought-provoking. Enjoy the ride."

—Kathy Tyers, author of the "Firebird" series, *Crystal Witness, Shivering World, One Mind's Eye,* and *Star Wars: The Truce at Bakura*

# Copyrights & Contents

## Best Speculative Fiction
by Christian Authors

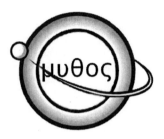

*Nothing but powerful short tales*

# Mythic Orbits 2016

# Editor's Introduction

You might be picking up this book wondering what in the world "Mythic Orbits 2016" refers to. I'm not sure if it will reassure you to tell you the name Mythic Orbits was simply intended to suggest both science fiction and fantasy and to identify this book in a distinctive way, along with any that follow after it in a series.

Yes, I would like to do this as a series, selecting excellent stories from upcoming years. So there will be a "Mythic Orbits 2017" and "Mythic Orbits 2018," and so on, if God allows that to be possible.

Ideally this collection would include the best stories published in a particular year, but that wasn't possible this time around. This collection of stories is tagged with 2016 in the title because that's the year of publication of this anthology, not of the individual stories within it (with a few exceptions).

Now that you understand the basic idea behind the title, I should mention that the suggestion of science fiction and fantasy it contains winds up being a bit incomplete. This anthology of 14 authors includes what we would have to call horror and paranormal stories as well as more definitive science fiction and fantasy. Please see "mythic" as covering these genres as well.

Just as this anthology represents a wide variety of genres, there is no single theme to these tales, though the subject of empathy or lack thereof does come up in them repeatedly. This is most definitely *not* an anthology about orbits which are somehow mythical.

What this *is* is a showcase for the best stories submitted to me in the general field of speculative fiction by Christian authors. Some I specifically solicited for stories because of my high opinion of other tales they wrote. I also put out a call for authors among all my social networks and had some authors suggested to me on a "friend (or acquaintance) of a friend" basis. Some authors represented here also came in from "out of the blue," people I had never met before, not even in the social media sense of "met."

I would have liked to cast the net even wider for these stories and hope to reach more authors in the future, but I received dozens of stories in response to my requests, giving me the chance to pick the best ones. I'm satisfied that I achieved my

# Editor's Introduction

goals for this anthology.

And the first among those goals was simply to demonstrate that Christian authors really *can* write speculative fiction well. Stories with a wide range of appeal are included here, mostly serious, some with humor, some with "happy endings" and others clearly not so happy. But my hope is you will find all of them worth reading.

I also hoped that some of the authors submitting to me would write using Christian themes and I wasn't disappointed. Though I never required that.

It so happens that some of these stories feature Christian characters in speculative fiction worlds, some make use of Christian themes either subtly or overtly, while some have no discernible connection to Christianity at all. Which again was along the lines of what I wanted —to showcase Christian *authors* rather than stories with deliberate Christian themes.

There was no specific content or doctrinal test for these tales, though it happens to be that they are basically clean. As long as the violence mentioned in a few of these stories wasn't portrayed too graphically, this collection would rate a PG in the US movie rating system for the suffering mentioned in a few of these tales and a few relatively mild words like "bastard." Sexuality in this anthology is limited to being attracted to someone...and a single story kiss.

In doctrine, these stories do what speculative fiction as a whole *does*—create worlds unlike our own and put the reader inside them. These stories do not assert these unreal situations are actually true...though things that are imaginary can reveal truths about what is real, of course. But nothing here overtly contradicts the Bible. Even strict interpretations that there cannot possibly be ghosts or fairies or certain particular monsters, which some of these tales include, could be harmonized simply by reinterpreting some of the stories as involving demons if a reader wished to do so.

These stories are not real (of course), but if God happened to make alternate universes, there is nothing in any of these stories which could not perhaps happen in some other world. Which does not mean these tales do not stretch the imagination or end in unexpected ways. I believe they do. I hope you agree with me as you read.

# Editor's Introduction

Travis Perry
Bear Publications
Monterrey, Mexico.  December 2016.

## The Bones Don't Lie
By Mark Venturini

Benshir jerked awake, his heart pounding, his skin slick with sweat despite the cold night air. He took a deep breath and rubbed his eyes, trying to shake off the ghosts of a shadowy, formless dream. It was about Timri again, wasn't it? He groped in the dark and through his own haunting dread for his little brother's mat.

Empty.

He saw a short figure standing before the open window, softly illuminated by the stars and setting moons. "Timri?"

The figure didn't move. Benshir struggled to his feet. A cold night breeze pricked his skin. "Ti?"

"Do you hear it?" Timri whispered,

Benshir touched Timri's shoulder and found his own hand trembling. "Hear what?"

Timri stirred. "Singing. Ain't it beautiful?"

Benshir's grasp tightened involuntarily. "A dream. Nothing more."

"No. I still hear it." Timri motioned with his head. "Out there."

Benshir peered into the frosty night,

seeing only the outlines of trees and hills that he'd known all his life. "I hear moonflies singing and the old wulla croaking down by the pond."

Timri sighed. "I hear people singing. Lots of people."

Benshir closed the shutters. "Come on, you're going back to bed before you freeze us to death." He led Timri to the mats and lay down close to him, pulling the thin covers over them both.

"Benshir?"

"Go to sleep, Ti."

"Ever heard singing like that?"
Benshir hesitated. "You were dreaming," he said, afraid to say any more.

Benshir awoke to pounding on the bedroom door. "Come on, you two," a husky voice called. "The day's wasting and we've got two fields to plow!"

Benshir groaned. Misty dawn already spilled into the room. "Right away, Father." No excuse for oversleeping.

Father poked his head into the room, gray stubble covering a weathered face. "You boys take the south field. I'll be in the north. I want three rows turned before breakfast."

The door closed. Three rows! Benshir's muscles ached at the thought. He lifted himself from the mat and saw Timri staring out the window, silent, unmoving.

"Hear anything, Ti?"

Timri's shoulders went up and then down. He took a deep frosty breath. "Not yet."

Benshir stepped beside him. "See, told you it was a dream. Nothing more."

"Maybe if I wait and listen harder—"

Benshir jabbed Timri away from the window. "Get your clothes on."

Benshir was quickly ready, but Timri sat staring at the window with only his breeches on. Benshir threw a shirt at him. "Come on pond-wart. Father wants three rows turned!"

Absently Timri buttoned his shirt and laced his boots. Before opening the door, Benshir grabbed Timri's shoulder and knelt. "What happened last night is our secret. Mother and Father needn't know."

"Why?"

"Planting and calving are plenty for them to tend to. No need to worry them with your dream." Benshir pushed open the door. "Agree?"

Reluctantly Timri nodded.

"Good."

They stepped from the cottage into the cold morning, their breath rising in white swirls. Damp mist hugged the house and barn and the entire valley. Trees and distant mountains appeared as vague outlines.

Timri stared at the mountains, the mountains their ancestors crossed from Old Nevarean generations before. Surprisingly, Benshir caught himself straining to listen. For what, he didn't know. Something, *anything* that could put a name to the faceless dread still scratching at his mind.

He heard nothing save for the birds rising from their beds.

"Get moving, you lazies," Father called as he led a large antlered buklak from the barn. "Can't do everything m'self."

Benshir shook himself. *Foolishness: dreams and singing and worry.* All this stupidity and work wasn't getting done. "Move it, Ti, before Father takes a switch to us."

When Timri didn't move, Benshir elbowed him toward the barn. "You get

Ezzy and I'll ready the plow. Go on."

Surprisingly, it wasn't long before Benshir saw Timri leading Ezzy through the mist. Quickly, they had the large lumbering buklak yoked to the plow. Benshir tried his best to guide the heavy, lurching plow as it cut through the stubborn sod.

The sun rose higher. Mist melted away, revealing blue sky and high craggy peaks still packed with snow. But there in the valley, the morning warmed and hinted of cruel afternoon heat. Sweat beaded Benshir's brow as he fought to keep the plow moving. The task proved impossible with Timri staring at the mountains instead of leading Ezzy.

Benshir slapped the plow handle. "I'm done with your nonsense, you little wart!"

Timri's face looked so innocent. "You don't hear it, do ya?"

"I'll tell you what I hear! I hear little Timri whimpering when I tell Father and he deals with your lazy hide!"

"You wouldn't!"

"I swear—"

"Breakfast, Benshir, Timri," Mother called from beyond the trees. "Come before you father eats it all."

# The Bones Don't Lie

Benshir looked at Timri, then at the field. They had only turned one row and Father wanted three. He wiped his face with his sleeve. "C'mon. Let's go eat. We'll make up the lost time after."

Timri started for the house, but Benshir turned him around. "Remember your promise. I don't want Mother and Father fretting about your nonsense."

Timri kept his promise. His gaze never strayed from his bowl while he ate his porridge.

"Aren't you two the silent ones this morning," Mother said.

Benshir glanced at her and realized he'd been staring at Timri. He took his first spoonful of porridge. "Sorry."

Mother smiled. "No need to apologize for a little peace and quiet."

Father broke off a piece of coarse bread from the dark loaf in the middle of the table. "So, how far you boys get?"

Benshir hesitated, facing the feared moment of truth.

"Three!" Timri jumped in. "Three, and near ready to start the fourth." He had the same stupid innocent look that Benshir saw in the field.

Benshir wanted to tear into that smug

face but held his tongue. Maybe this time it was good that his parents didn't see through Ti's games.

Father gave an approving nod and bit into the bread. "Guess I'll see the entire field turned by supper."

And he did. As the sun brushed the tops of the western peaks, Benshir and Timri cut through the last row of sod. Father patted each son on the shoulder as they led Ezzy to the barn. "Lot of work boys. You both did good. I'm proud of you both."

"I'll take Ezzy," Timri said.

Benhir watched Timri lead the buklak into the barn. Timri *had* worked hard turning the field, but Benshir knew that fear of the switch was the true reason— nothing more, nothing less.

That night Benshir collapsed exhausted on his mat. Despite falling instantly into a deep sleep, his dream came again along with gnawing dread.

In his dream, he saw hundreds of distant faceless figures moving and flowing in incomprehensible patterns until they formed dozens of long straight ranks. The figures all seemed to wait in their ridged stance, watching and listening.

15

Then he heard a child's voice, Timri's voice.

Benshir jumped awake. Outside, the cold moons still shown bright, softly illuminating a small figure at the window.

"Ti?" Benshir whispered, his voice shaky.

Timri turned. "The singing's getting louder."

The sun slowly crossed the afternoon sky, dancing with the few clouds drifting past. Benshir swung the ax with a quick fluid motion and split the log with a single swipe. But as the blade cut deep, he didn't hear splintering wood, only the dark lingering dread from all his dreams.

He had the ax moving again in a high arc when he heard hoof beats. Six men sporting long red capes approached from the direction of Nevarean, *Priests!*

Benshir let the ax bite hard into the log as the priests reined in their cawals, long-necked beasts already molting in the warm spring air. "Whose farm is this?" the center red-cape asked.

Benshir faltered. "Urrbale." Then louder—"Pimor and Sarria Urrbale."

"Is the master here?"

"My father's behind the barn. My mother and brother are gathering mushrooms and roots."

"Go fetch your father."

Benshir ran to the barn and led his father toward the priests, a scythe in his grasp. Father stiffened. "Benshir, go to the house."

"The boy will stay," the priest said. He nudged his cawal forward. "Our apologies for the intrusion."

Father laid down the scythe and bowed with hands outstretched. "My home is yours, Father," he said, his wary voice darkening the formal greeting.

The priest bowed his gaunt, chiseled face. "We are on a quest and we need assistance from both of you."

Father's eyes narrowed. "For what?"

The priest dismounted. The others did the same. "The Eternal Lord has stirred the Bones."

"How does this concern my family?"

"It has been revealed to me that the Shafiu are on the move," the priest said darkly. "They seek Nevarean again."

Benshir glanced at his father. "What does this mean?"

# The Bones Don't Lie

"Haven't you taught your son anything of our past?" the priest said impatiently to Father. Then to Benshir—"The Shafiu need a Channel to find us, someone they can touch and hold with their witchery to guide them here."

He motioned behind him and two priests stepped forward, each carrying a richly engraved wooden box. "The Lord commands the Channel be found and cut off for the safety of Nevarean."

Father tensed and blocked the priests. "And the Lord revealed to me that you must leave my farm."

"Do you mock me?" the head priest barked.

"Never, Father. I only question the message you thought you heard," Benshir's father replied in a surprisingly calm, cool voice. "You'll find nothing here."

The priest's lips pinched into a smirk.

"That is yet to be determined."

The boxes were opened. From one the priest took the top half of a bleached feral skull, empty eye sockets staring above a long snout. From the other he drew the lower jaw, rows of teeth still protruding. He brought both halves close together.

"We are all in danger until the Bones

reveal the Channel to us."

The two halves quivered and practically jumped from the priest's hands to fuse together. The priest laid the fused skull on the ground, bowed his head, and raised his hands to the sky.

The priest began to chant as his companion priests bowed their heads. "Eternal Lord guide us . . . We entreat thee . . . Show us . . ."

Benshir realized he was holding his breath. Would the skull speak? Would lightning fall or fire leap from the ground? Did the eye sockets flash red? The priest slowly turned his head from side to side, apparently listening. To what? The wind? Bugs buzzing around?

*To singing?*

The priest lowered his arms. "I cannot sense the Channel yet. It is still too early in the search." He took a frustrated breath and retrieved the skull, placing each half in its box. "In which direction do your neighbors live?"

Father didn't move and he didn't speak.

"Now," the priest demanded. "We have little time."

Father glared. "The Rumms, beyond

19

the western knoll. Old man Jul across Oma Creek, about a half-day distant."

The priest mounted his cawal. "Thank you for your patience, Master Urrbale." He pulled the reins. "We may be back. One never knows where the Bones will lead. Time is short, though. Of that I'm certain." He turned his beast and the six priests headed west, red capes flapping behind them.

That night the family sat around the hearth. "Priests came to the farm today," Father said, lighting his pipe.

Mother put a hand to her chest and glanced nervously at the door. "What did they want?"

"Looking for something," Father replied. He bit his pipe stem. Embers glowed red in the small bowl. "Whatever it was, they didn't find it here."

"Who are the Shafiu, Father?" Timri asked.

Mother shifted in her chair, quickly trying to hide the concern that Benshir noticed flicker in her eyes. "How do you know about the Shafiu?" she asked.

Timri hesitated, then shrugged. "I hear

you and Father talk about them sometime."

Benshir cringed at Timri's stupid innocent look. "Shut up, pond-wart. No need to dig up things that don't concern you."

"Hmm, don't recall talking about the Shafiu before," Father said. He blew out a wisp of smoke. "The priest did bark at me up and down for not telling our past. Maybe he's right. The boys are old enough."

He examined his pipe. "Many generations ago, our ancestors, the Maujeen, ruled the Western Reaches as kings and queens. Another race, the Shafiu, lived alongside us. They were a dirty, heathen race far below the station of the Maujeen. Over many generations we conquered them and they became our slaves."

Father stared at the hearth. "Oh, we were a wicked people then, brutal, and the Shafiu suffered greatly. But the people of Old Nevarean saw the brutality and tried the way of peace. They learned the way of brotherhood and did everything possible to shed their wicked ways. Old Nevarean actually became a haven for escaping Shafiu."

"What then?" Timri asked.

Father shook his head. "The people of Old Nevarean became the persecuted, just as the Shafiu. But the Ancient Ones' belief in peace was too strong. Instead of fighting, they fled the city. Nearly a thousand souls escaped the persecution and fled high into the mountains where the cold and snow nearly finished them. But the higher they climbed, the less the Maujeen chased them. Finally, the hunting stopped."

"Why?"

"The priests learned through their arts that the Shafiu rebelled and a bloody war was fought. The Eternal Lord revealed through the Bones that the Shafiu killed the Maujeen, and those not killed were made slaves."

"That's when the Old Ones found this valley over eight generations ago, right Father?" Benshir asked.

"Yes," Father said. "We found a new home here. We found peace."

"The priests are right," Mother said. "We have no part in the outside world any more. We're happy here and safe."

Father drew at the sweet aroma in his pipe, exhaled. "I will protect this valley, our

Nevarean, with my life. We won't run again."

"Will it come to that?" Benshir asked.

Father shrugged. "The priests have always warned the Shafiu still hunt the last of the Maujeen, the last of their old enemy. Our people from Old Nevarean helped them, but they don't remember that. Old hate will never die unless the Shafiu bury it."

"Stop this nonsense!" Mother said. "You're scaring Timri."

"No I'm not," Father replied. "Said Timri is old enough and so he is. Aren't you son?"

Benshir slapped Timri's knee when he saw a hint of doubt in his brother's eyes. "Nobody's found us yet. They won't find us now."

Father rose and tapped his pipe against the hearth. "Best for us to go to bed. Got to start planting tomorrow."

Benshir scooped Timri into his arms. "We'll be ready at first light."

"That's what I like to hear. Good night to you both."

Grabbing a candle, Benshir carried Timri into the bedroom. "Aren't you scared?" Timri whispered after Benshir closed the door.

"Nope. Nobody's found us after all these years and nobody ever will. The Lord will protect."

"First time you've ever mentioned the Lord," Timri replied.

"Maybe it's time I did, Ti. Get ready for bed."

"But—"

"Now, pond-wart."

Timri didn't move. Benshir blew out the candle and slipped under his cover. "Fine. Stand there all night."

Benshir heard Timri open the window shutters followed by the patter of rain outside. "Shut the window, idiot. You'll get soaked."

"You don't hear the singing," Timri said. It wasn't a question.

"No."

"Benshir, I'm scared."

Benshir went to his brother and drew him close. "You're safe with me." He closed the shutters and led Timri to bed. His arms didn't leave Timri until he heard the deep even breaths of sleep.

Try as he might, Benshir couldn't sleep. He lay staring through the dark at the memory of his own dreams, listening through the silence for the mysterious singing only Timri could hear. Slowly, though, as the night wore on and rain continued to fall, fatigue started to dull Benshir's mind and sleep to darken his eyes.

They weren't alone in the room. Benshir jerked awake in the dark. "Father?"

Silence.

Benshir's heart froze. A form glided across the room. Tall and black, so dark it stood out against the lighter night. The form looked like a black head upon a solid black body without arms or legs. Whispers swirled around the creature.

*"Guide us."*

*"Show us the Channel."*

*"We beseech thee. Help us find the Channel."*

The black form crept alongside Timri's mat. Timri groaned and thrashed about. Benshir threw himself against his brother. Timri cried out, struggling against the weight.

Benshir slapped his hand against Timri's mouth. "Shhh. Don't move." His eyes darted around the room. No shadow, no movement. He held his breath and strained to listen. The room remained silent save for Timri's labored breathing.

"We can't stay," Benshir whispered. He slid his hand from Timri's mouth.

"You hurt me," Timri cried.

"Shhh!" Benshir hissed. He groped around until he found their clothes. "Get dressed. Hurry."

"Why—"

"Now, pond-wart."

Benshir fumbled with his clothes and boots in the dark. He grabbed Timri's shirt and then Timri. They ran from the house into stinging sleet. Benshir's breath caught in the sudden biting air. Timri sobbed as Benshir put him down.

"This is a hiding game," Benshir whispered. "I played it with Father before you were born. If he doesn't find us before breakfast, we win the game and he gives us sweets."

Benshir rubbed Timri's arms and helped him with his shirt. "If Father wins, we don't get any sweets. Want to play?"

Timri shivered hard and shook his head. "I'm freezing. I want to go in."

Benshir fastened Timri's last button.

He tried to calm his voice. "If we go in, we lose the game."

"You sound scared."

Benshir wiped his eyes. "I don't want to lose the game. C'mon."

He dragged Timri past the barn and into the woods. Driving sleet stung his skin like hundreds of Mother's sewing needles. He ducked behind a dirt mound and held Timri's shivering body close. Soon he was shivering too from cold and damp seeping deep into his bones. Timri choked back sobs. "You're doin' fine, Ti," Benshir whispered next to his ear. "We're going to win this game."

Benshir could see part of the house through the fading night. Father burst from the house into the gloom followed by Mother. "Benshir! Timri!" Father shouted. "Get your lazy hides back inside the house!"

Timri tried pushing away but Benshir held him down. "He can't find us before breakfast. Those are the rules."

Mother held her tattered coat tight to her neck, frantically searching around the house. "Timri? Benshir? Come inside. You'll catch your death in this weather."

"They'll catch my grief unless this

foolishness stops now," Father roared before disappearing into the barn.

"He sounds really mad," Timri whimpered.

"It's part of the game."

"They're not here," Mother cried.

Father ran from the barn. "I'm going to beat those boys!"

The rumble of hooves broke through the rain. A cawal charged through the gloom, the mounted priest's blood-red cape billowing. More priests followed, and then ten Nevarean guards in dull metal helm and breastplate, long spears pointing to the slate gray sky.

The lead priest pulled hard on the reins. "Where is he? The Channel is here. The Bones don't lie."

Father retrieved an ax from the barn and ran to Mother's side. "You're trespassing. Leave now!"

"One of your sons is the Channel," the priest growled, jumping from his saddle. "Search the farm! The Bones don't lie!"

All riders dismounted. "One in the house," a Nevarean guard ordered. "One in the barn. The rest start searching the fields."

Timri's body trembled next to Benshir. "This ain't no game, is it?"

Crouching, Benshir grabbed Timri. They were both shaking, but Benshir knew he had to be strong and brave for Timri, everything he didn't feel. Carefully, he backed away from the mound. Then they ran.

Their escape was slow. They had to be quiet. Stones and tangled roots hid beneath leaves and hazy morning light, ready to trip anyone careless. Benshir stopped often, listening for any sounds.

The deeper they ran into the woods, the deeper Timri withdrew into himself. He stared at the distant shadowed mountains until Benshir had to shake him to keep moving. "Don't stop, Ti," he pleaded. "Keep moving, Ti . . . Help me, Ti."

Finally, Timri turned to Benshir, his dark hair plastered against his forehead, his gaze seemingly somewhere else. "Where are we going?"

"Don't know. Somewhere, anywhere away from Nevarean. There's some caves in the hills past old Jul's place."

"Can't we go home? I want to go home."

"Soon. I promise."

The rain stopped and the day brightened as they approached a narrow field of tall grass and spring flowers. They crouched at the tree line and waited. Gurgling water nearby was the only sound. There were no hoof beats, no shouts. Maybe they were safe. "C'mon, Ti," Benshir said.

They crossed the field with the sound of water growing louder and came to the bank of the swollen Oma Creek. Panic struck Benshir as he watched the angry churning water slap the boulders. "I think there's a place to cross further down. Let's go."

Timri clutched his ears and staggered at the water's edge. Benshir's heart skipped several beats. He lunged and pulled Timri back before he could fall in. "It's so loud, Benshir," Timri muttered. "Can't you hear it?"

"There they are!" a male voice shouted. "I command you to stop in the name of the High Priest of Nevarean!"

Benshir spun. Priests and guards charged across the field, red capes flowing and bows made ready.

Benshir took a hesitant step into the

rushing water, sending freezing bolts of pain through his leg.

"Don't be a fool!" the lead priest shouted.

Then he saw a wagon lumbering across the field driven by a Nevarean guard. Two people sat in back. "My babies!" Mother shrieked. "Don't touch my babies!"

The lead priest jumped from his cawal, holding a bleached skull with red fire churning inside its eye sockets. "The Bones don't lie! The Shafiu want to destroy the village and you're helping them!"

Guards surrounded Benshir and Timri with nocked arrows ready to strike. "Which one of you is the Channel?" the priest demanded.

"Stop!" Father shouted from the approaching wagon. Were his wrists bound with chains? "You can't believe my sons are involved!"

"I am a priest of the Eternal Lord. I am oath-bound to believe," the priest shot back. "I am oath-bound to protect Nevarean. Every day I pray for guidance. Every day I listen and follow where my heart leads. All for the sake of the people." Father's voice cracked. "My sons are innocent! You're all mad!"

# The Bones Don't Lie

The priest glared at Benshir. "Mad?" he roared. "Nevarean is in danger while the Channel lives!"

"Kill me instead," Father pleaded.

"They're just children," Mother bawled.

"The Channel is always a child," the priest answered, his voice as cold as any winter night. He pointed the skull between Timri and Benshir. "Eternal Lord, use the Bones to guide us. Reveal to us the Channel . . ."

The skull shuddered to life. It jerked left and then right. Benshir held his breath as it slowly pointed at Timri.

Benshir jumped in front of his brother. "I'm the Channel! I had the dreams! I—"

A bowstring snapped. An arrow ripped into Benshir's chest. He staggered back and collapsed.

Freezing water swirled around him. Bone-crushing cold jolted his body, joining with the searing fire of pain raging in his chest.

"Benshir!" Timri cried.

"My boy!" someone screamed from far away.

Suddenly Benshir heard it, coming

from the mountains, coming from beyond Timri's sobs and his mother's cries. He heard singing, a huge beautiful chorus. *"We are the Shafiu and we seek our friends of Nevarean . . ."*

Violent shudders rocked Benshir's body as rising icy water bit his ears and cheeks. *"We honor our ancient friends, you who showed us the way of peace."*

The churning current pried Benshir from the boulders. *"Join us people of Nevarean. Shafiu and Maujeen have lived in peace for many generations . . ."*

Strong hands dragged Benshir from the water's numbing grip. Timri fell to his knees. "Get up, Benshir! Please get up!"

The priest knelt next to Benshir. "Do you hear it?" Benshir muttered. He coughed salty blood and burning bile. *"Join us people of Nevarean . . ."* He moved his arm, shooting spasms of pain through his body, and grasped the priest's wrist, "Do you?"

Surprise flicked across the priest's face and then his eyes widened in horror as he lifted his face toward the mountains. He jerked his arm away and stumbled back. "What did you do to me?"

A blanket of numbness spread over

Benshir's body. He forced his lips to move. "Do you hear it?"

It appeared the priest hadn't heard the question until he finally said, "Yes." He nodded in wonderment and continued to stare at the mountains. "Yes . . . All these years, how could we have been so wrong? How could we have misinterpreted this?"

A shadow moved along the edge of Benshir's vision. "My Father, the Channel must be dealt with."

The priest's fear flashed to anger. "Don't harm the little one!" He staggered back to Benshir. "Help him! Tend to his wounds!"

*"We are the Shafiu and we seek our friends of Nevarean . . ."*

Benshir's world dimmed and the beautiful music faded. Somewhere, somehow, he heard the priest's distant voice. "The Bones. The Bones. Eternal Lord save us! How could we have been so blind?"

### End

**Mark Venturini's** short fiction and flash fiction has appeared in various print and electronic magazines over the years. He founded the Pittsburgh East Scribes critique group in 2010 with the aim of helping aspiring writers pursue their dream of publication. The group has flourished beyond his wildest dreams.

When he's not exploring fantastical realms, you'll find Mark exploring the natural wonders of South Western PA either in his kayak or with a backpack slung over his shoulders.

## The Disembodied Hand
By Jill Domschot

I ascended into the light from my basement, from the smell of damp cement, as if a river ran through it, into the odor of fog. The sun rose over the actual river, and it hovered with me face-to-face. I had suffered from a migraine for days, and I was tired of hiding in the dark. But the fresh morning air only made it worse.

I walked a few paces down the brick riverwalk, jaw tight to quell nausea. At the peak of blinding pain, I tried to evacuate the sun from my head. With my hands pressed at my temples, I extinguished it— the light, everything. Darkness plummeted.

"Hello?" I called out. "Somebody help me, please?"

I sensed a presence near me, smelled sweat and tobacco and alcohol: a person who hadn't showered for a long time. Perhaps a man who had been out all last night. And now it was night again, at least from my perspective. My body stiffened, which occurs in darkness.

"Do you need help?" His voice hacked roughly.

"I can't see anything. Can you see

anything?" The wind off the river rattled my insides and shook my voice. "Can you help me?"

"You want me to call an ambulance?" he asked. "You on drugs?"

"Migraine drugs."

He made the call; I heard his rough voice speak. He touched my shoulder, or I assumed he did, because a burning smell crept inside my mind. He was smoking.

"What exactly is the matter with you?" he asked.

"I can't see. Thirty seconds ago, the sun was rising, and now everything's dark."

He repeated my words. He further interrogated me and again reiterated my inadequate answers. I reached for him and found his sleeve and plucked at it with my fingers.

"All right," he said, and he pried my fingers from his shirt. "They're sending an ambulance. Let's go sit. I'll help you to the bench, and we'll wait together." He took my hand, and I felt led: sheep to slaughter or back to the flock?

I didn't belong to a flock. With my hand loose in his palm, I could slip away in a stroke. So I clenched his hand, and he must have found comfort in it as so many others did because he suddenly moaned at me and told me his story. He had been drinking all night, was still a little drunk, he informed me. He drank too much, lost his girlfriend, got in a fight.

I listened, and that was my place, not part of the flock, but the world's confessor, even if the circumstances didn't call for it. Didn't I need a confessor this time? He was drunk and sad, but I was blind.

The ambulance screamed silently up the street, and I saw it because he articulated the details, the swirling lights, mute sirens. The engine idled nearby. Through the ensuing confusion of questions, I lost the man's hand and I didn't know if he was far or near, whether he wandered away to nurse his hangover or chose to stay by my side.

No, I wasn't diabetic, and my sight was perfect less than an hour ago. I suffered migraines, and I swallowed painkillers by the handful, and that was all. They checked my vitals. I was fine, except for blindness. All except for that minor detail, I was perfect. They led me to the ambulance: led again, and surrounded by darkness, and trusting the volley of voices.

I heard a gruff voice, and a conflicting stream of odors surged around my head. "Come with me," I yelled to my rescuer, and I couldn't separate him from the others. I didn't know if he was there, but a man's hand latched onto mine, and the hand remained in mine during transport. Wheeling through darkness caused seasickness. But I wasn't a complainer. I was a pill-swallower, instead.

The man stayed by my side once in the hospital, and his voice softened, and his scent sweetened from the harsh of cigarettes and hard alcohol to that of exotic cigars and wine. He mingled with me through the signing of paperwork I couldn't read and the brain scan I couldn't detect. It was a tumor, the man explained to me, a tumor that pressed against my optic nerve. And he explained the risks of removing it.

Before the others could drug me for surgery, I asked him about God because I was afraid of going into surgery blind.

"I believe," he said.

"I don't. I don't know how to believe."

"I'm sorry." His voice was low with grief. A man who obliterated his nights in alcohol grieved for me.

# The Disembodied Hand

"I only want what everybody wants. Non-attachment," I whispered, but they drugged me at that point, and I lost touch and slipped away. My words garbled themselves in a tangled knot of nonsense.

"I can't attach–God I can't attach to. Can't play." But I meant pray.

"Lamb on the throne, shepherd to men, rescue your lost," he prayed for me, but his sound waves eventually disappeared along with everything else.

Later, when time returned, I opened my eyes halfway, and the light broke through my retinas.

"Oh, you're awake." A woman wearing scrubs peered down at me, blocking the intense light source. "How are you feeling?"

"Where'd the man go?" I asked her, my throat dry and raspy. Did I really believe he would wait for my recovery? Yes, I did. I believed.

"What man?" she asked.

"The man who brought me here."

"The EMTs? You can thank them later."

"No, the man who rode with me and helped me sign the paperwork."

"I helped you sign the paperwork," she

said.

Her sensical rebuttal stymied me. I searched for words. "The man who prayed with me before surgery."

"Oh. Maybe I should call for the doctor. Hallucinations aren't a good sign." My head lolled over the pillows. "The man who held my hand." My lips sagged strangely, and the words dripped from my mouth.

"There was no man," she said, nurse-knows-best, and she padded away in her hospital shoes.

When I looked after her, my periphery restored, the light glowed at me, locked deep within the waxen floors. I imagined the man I couldn't see standing in the light. They'd explained the risks to me before surgery, and he'd helped me comprehend their words: permanent nerve damage possible. Permanent damage to the optic nerve possible because of the tumor and the delicacy of removing it. But the sight I needed most could be forever damaged by daylight's return, and how had the man failed to warn me?

End

# The Disembodied Hand

**Jill Domschot** is a writer consumed with ideas. Although these ideas often spawn absurd and/or dark and twisted stories, they are just as likely to compel her to create collations and catalogs. She's a wife, a mom of four, and currently the author of two books: a collection of fantasy, sci fi and magical realist shorts, *The Jaybird's Nest and other Stories*; and a metaphysical tale about a woman, a man, a dragon and a child, *Anna and the Dragon*. For work that actually pays, she edits and formats books for a wide variety of authors.

For more, go to her website, jdomschot@msn.com.

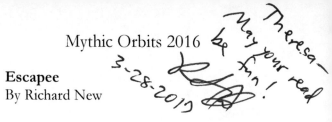

Theresa—
May your read
fun!
3-28-2019

## Escapee
By Richard New

I awake with a sense of nothing. However, something must have gone wrong with ship's power, including the backup generators. The lights are out. The cell's locks have unlocked.

Weightless. Something *really* went wrong.

I float out of the brig into the corridor. The air is still. Nothing blowing from the vents.

Where's the crew? More important, where's their blasters?

I move toward the stern and find a closed mid-ship airlock. I look through the port in the door and can just make out a suit. Stitched on the suit's breast pocket is the name Perry. The suit is occupied—except for the missing helmet and head.

Two frozen jets of bubbled blood point away from the neck. What a waste.

Behind the dead crewmember, I see star-scape rolling by where there should be more ship. Jagged metal points in the direction the ship rolls. Something hit us and cut the ship in two.

I turn in the weightless corridor and

see I'm at the lifeboat junction. Both lifeboat ports—one to either side—are empty.

*Great.* I'm alone. The crew, my jailers, abandoned me.

I move toward the control deck, checking all compartments for the four hand blasters and the two rifle blasters.

After all, I might want to kill myself. End it all.

I find no blasters. Nor food.

Cold. Hungry.

All power in the ship is dead. No comm.

I sit in one of the two seats. One is the commander's position; the other is the pilot's. I don't know which is which. Nor do I care.

I watch the stars roll by out the forward viewports.

I wait.

Hungry.

Wait! Out the forward viewport. What

was that?

A star's blotted out. Then several more. Something's out there. Another ship?

More rotation until the angle is right for Sol to light up whatever it is for me to see.

It is a ship! A different and weird ship. Not a ship from Earth, anyway. Massive section—that's the engine, I think.

Something crouches in its open airlock. Maneuvering jets thrust, pulling the object towards me.

I put on a spare suit. Energize it. Step to the nearest airlock. Cycle the outer door open.

I wait.

I hear scrabbling noises. The airlock cycles.

I pick up a spanner from the toolbox on my side of the lock and wait.

A spacesuit steps on board my ship. I come down on top of it with the spanner. The spanner connects to the part of the suit nearest me and drives it to the deck. The rest of the suit tumbles over, pulling the part I smashed down along with it. It smacks against the far corridor wall—upside down. The suit does not move.

# Escapee

Curious. The hands ... have six digits each. As do the ... feet. No boots on the feet. All four appendages wear gloves with six digits.

Not from this neighborhood. I wonder what inspired it come aboard? To help? Decision time. Stay or go?

I bundle the occupied suit against me with one hand. Cycle outside. A little four-handled tug is tethered by the airlock. I remove the tether from the tug and use it to tie the occupied suit to me. I grab two of the pipe shaped handles. Between the two opposing handle sets, there is a T-shaped handle shoved to one side of a slot. No other controls. What looks like a fuel tank is below the T handle. Reaction motors below that.

I shove the T handle to the slot's other side and grab two of the handles.

Below me, motors fire and I head toward the other ship.

I see no movement within the view-ports of the other ship. As I get nearer, the tug matches the non-rotation of its mother ship.

I step off into the alien airlock. There is no port to view inside the ship. I untie the occupied suit and tether it to a hook inside the lock.

The little tug moves off to one side of the airlock and installs itself in a niche.

I study the airlock control.

There is a blinking, circular, red light above a non-lit light in the airlock wall. I push the blinking red light.

Nothing happens.

I push the non-blinking light.

The non-lit light is now a blinking green light. The outer airlock door closes. My suit deflates slightly as air pressure builds up. I ready my spanner. The inner airlock door opens.

I wait.

A hairy "head" with three eyes in a row looks into the airlock.

I swing the spanner.

Both aliens are unconscious, I think, but breathing. I've removed the one from its spacesuit and tied both into what pass for beds, or cots, in this ship. Fortunately, the air does not smell too bad.

I search for food the aliens would eat and find what looks like plastic-wrapped food bars. I sniff at one. Odd smell, a

Escapee

touch of curry and cinnamon.

*Yuck.*

I tour the alien ship and find nothing that looks like a weapon. The ship is long. Starting from the flight deck at the front, there is an encircling common space used as galley / storage / dorms — where I restrained both Three-eyes on cots, two escape pods opposite each other, and an odd shaped section connecting with the antenna array. There a few scattered spaces equipped with odd-looking equipment— science instruments?

There is a tiny triangle shaped room with an image of what looks like a suffering alien on a Y-shaped post.

A prayer space? A place to bend the knee? The Earth ship had nothing like it.

The massive engine section at the rear finishes the ship.

But I'm no longer gonna be hungry. I've secured food for myself.

The control board where the two aliens control the craft is strange. Only two controls on a central panel. A purple light is blinking at one end of a glass-filled slot. Another T handle rests against its stop in another slot. Circular glass surrounds the T handle control.

I move the T handle to the other end of its slot.

The purple light starts extending itself across the glass-filled slot. At the same time, I notice stars outside moving left to right. The ship is rotating—one hundred and eighty degrees?

The rotation stops. Has the ship reversed its heading? The purple light is now blinking at the other end of the glass-filled slot.

A thin, orange line appears at the outer rim of the circular glass around the T handle. I feel a rumbling building from the rear of the ship. Orange light creeps across half of the glass circle.

I buckle myself best I can into one of the two forward facing seats. These seats don't feel right. Alien.

Orange light fills the glass circle. Outside the forward viewport, all the stars stretch into lines, as they coalesce into a single, bright point, dead ahead.

Field-folding technology?

I awake hungry. The bright point of light is still ahead. Cascades of bubbling

# Escapee

blue and white lighting swirls around the ship as we travel through space/time. I wonder where the ship is going. Perhaps to the Three-eye's home planet? Will some device of theirs warn them about an alien invader, me? Will the Three-eyes blow us up—send us to meet their Maker?

I return to the aliens. Both are jabbering at each other and me. Each of their three eyes are wide with some emotion.

I stoop down next to the first alien, the one that came to my ship. I bite its neck and suck. There is a lot of iron in their blood. Twice that of the humans I've fed on since the change.

Umm, a touch of curry and cinnamon. Nice.

## End

**Richard New** is a believer in Jesus Christ and a long time reader of science fiction. After thirty-five plus years, Richard is still married to the love of his life, Carle. They have a son and a daughter, and are the proud grandparents of two grandsons.

He has been published in Lines South, the quarterly publication of the Atlantic Coast Line and Seaboard Air Line Railroads Historical Society magazine (Vol. 32, No.1, pages 34 – 38). Splickety Publishing's Lightning blog of December 22, 2015 has his story: Patrol Duty.

You can read Richard's author blog at:

www.Facebook.com/Richard-New-1650222931906791

And his personal bladder cancer blog at:www.beginningcancer.wordpress.com

**Nether Ore**
By Kirk Outerbridge

He awoke.

Pain.

Skin burning like fire. He tried to scream but realized he had no breath. His eyes opened to a murky blur of blackness and hazy green light. Instantly he regretted it, his eyes stinging with a sharp caustic burn. He closed them, but it did nothing to lessen the searing pain.

Breathe.

He couldn't breathe!

His body reacted in a spasm, and he felt the strong resistance of water against his skin. He was floating...no, drowning. His kicked his legs, and his foot touched something solid. A rocky bottom? He pivoted, his foot clinging to the bottom like an anchor clinging for dear life. Near instinctively he pushed upward, and his head broke the surface.

Air filled his lungs and then exited twice as quickly with a sharp cough. The sound of heavy rain falling filled his ears with a hiss and battered his body in a sting that felt like hail. He reopened his eyes to the stinging blur. It was dark, wherever he was.

He was naked too, knee-deep in a body of dark water that stretched toward a horizon he could barely see. A blackened sky was overhead, so dark he couldn't even tell if there were clouds or not. But there had to be for the downpour that continued to fall like sheets of ice from the sky.

His skin was still aflame. He tried to wash himself in the rain to remove whatever it was that was burning his skin, but it seemed to only make it worse. He took a shaky step out of the water toward the shoreline a few feet away. He felt weak, tired. He wanted to sleep for a thousand years and wake up somewhere else. His feet protested with each step, hard granite shale digging painfully into his soles. The pain made him move faster, only to increase the pain with each step.

When he finally stepped out of the lapping surf, he all but collapsed onto the shore. More pain as the rocky gravel dug into his side and back. He cried out.

"Oy!"

That wasn't his cry.

He forced his eyes open in the burning rain, directed them to the sound. He lifted his head and saw a dull green glow coming from above. He rubbed his eyes, ignored the burning, and forced them to focus.

A figure stood over him, silhouetted against the dark sky. A lumpy and shapeless form. A dull green glow came from a single eye at where a head should be.

He jerked back in horror and let out another scream.

"Take it easy!" A hand reached out and snatched him by the arm. The figure lowered and the green eye became the torch of a miner's hat. The face beneath it was grizzled and worn. But it was human. The grizzly man frowned. "How did you get out here beyond the wall?"

The words made no sense.

"Did you fall?" The old man studied him with pale gray eyes. "Where's your coat? You'll burn up out here!"

Yes. Burn. He did burn.

The man leaned back and pulled him up off the rocky ground. "Got to get you inside. What's your name?"

Name...did he have a name?

"John..." he said.

The grizzly man stared at him for a second more. "You're fragged, ain't ya? You just reinstated?"

54

John tried his voice again. "I…I don't…" It took all his might to stop his jaw from trembling in the cold yet burning rain. "…know what you mean."

"Come on."

The grizzly man opened his coat and threw half of it over him and then threw his arm about John's waist. Grizzly carried him in a quick march away from the water's edge.

In moments John saw a large structure towering over them, reaching into the sky. A flat-roofed structure made of weather-worn concrete, dark and eerie in the faint green glow of Grizzly's single miner's lamp. It was a wall—at least a hundred feet high and stretching in each direction as far as the dim light would let him see.

Grizzly walked John toward an open hatchway at the base of the wall. The hatch looked like something that belonged in a submarine. He stepped through and then pulled John over the metal threshold before swinging the heavy door shut with a dull clang.

The man spent a minute or so cranking down on a hand wheel on the inside of the hatch, making sure it was secure before helping John again. They passed through the interior of the wall, a good ten yards thick, before reaching another open hatchway on the other side.

Grizzly helped him out and into an area filled with a still-faint, but stronger, glow of green light. The rain was still falling, but the wind was against the wall, and it formed a natural barrier overhead, the rain sweeping by far above them. The reprieve from the rain gave his eyes a chance to recover and to take in his new surrounds.

They were at the base of what felt like a dam. He could see now that the wall stretched for about a hundred yards each way and then embedded itself into the sides of a rocky canyon wall. Against the canyon walls was a double row of five story concrete block buildings that formed a square around an empty area that recessed into the ground about six feet or so. The rain filled the bottom square and reflected the sickly pale green glow of tiny windows that dotted the blocky buildings.

In the center of the square were two towering derrick cranes that looked centuries old. Lattice-framed booms lay idle. Empty cabs where the operator would sit were fashioned from corrugated zinc that was rusted a burnt red from the salt and rain. Next to the cranes were two enormous transparent plastic pipes that had to be over a yard in diameter each. They lay flat on the ground and ran perpendicular to the wall, with an upturned opening at the end that made them look like two giant tobacco pipes.

Grizzly took him by the arm and led him toward one of the concrete buildings. A few people emerged onto the square, all dressed in the same yellow raincoats as Grizzly wore and sporting the miner's hats with the single green lights. The man rapped on yet another hatch-like door in the side of the building.

A grinding of metal preceded the hatch swinging inward and a face poking out. It was a gaunt man who looked to be in his fifties, with a balding head combed over with a wisp of black hair. He didn't say anything, but studied John for a second before shooting a demanding stare for explanation at Grizzly.

"Found him beyond the sea wall," Grizzly said. "Looks fragged to me."

The man studied him with pale blue eyes. "What's your name?"

"John," he said.

"John what?"

He thought for a moment. "I don't know."

The man behind the hatch released a sigh. "Probably a reject from the rein-statement chamber. Jefferson is always trying to push boundaries with his memory reforms."

"Want me take him to Dr. Jefferson then, Doc?" Grizzly asked.

"No, don't bother," Blue Eyes said. "Get him fixed up at the infirmary and then take him with you to the mines." He paused a moment to give John a quick up and down. "No sense wasting a perfectly good body. Get him to work."

The infirmary was another hatch-accessible room across the concrete square where yet another doctor-like figure, this one wearing a white raincoat instead of a yellow one, slathered John in a greasy liquid that in no time seemed to ease the burning of his skin.

"This will help you rest," the doctor said before jabbing a needle into his shoulder.

The pain was sharp and was the last thing John remembered before drifting to the floor in sleep.

John stepped into the living room, sunlight beaming through the open sliding glass door, the curtains swaying with a gentle breeze, a blue horizon beyond. Toy blocks, a fire engine, and a fleet of tiny race cars littered the shag carpet floor.

A thunder of tiny footfalls came from an adjacent hallway, seconds before a pair of bronze-skinned boys in green shorts and matching tank tops stormed into the room to attack the toys. The older one looked to be about five, with close-cut ginger hair and a boisterous laugh. The younger was about two, slightly darker skinned, with thick black hair that curled into shoulder-length locks.

"Sam, Josh…stop running, please!" A second set of footfalls came, louder but more graceful.

A slender woman with deep chestnut skin and flowing ebony hair entered the room chasing after the boys. John stared at her for what seemed an eon, studying her dancer-like physique clad in baggy shorts and a loose fitting white tee. Her light grey eyes beamed like emeralds in the sun.

Karen… Karen was her name.

Neither she nor the boys seemed to notice him at first, but when she finally did look in his direction, she smiled. "You're back."

John tried to speak, but for some reason he couldn't.

"Go say hi to daddy."

Both boys turned about, and their faces lit up with recognition and excitement. They let out squeals of delight and rushed—

"Wake up now..."

John stirred and opened his eyes to the sickly green light of Grizzly's miner lamp shining into his face. Remnants of his dream evaporated all too quickly, and Grizzly tossed a pair of grey coveralls and a yellow raincoat next to him on the infirmary bed.

The old man handed him a spoon and bowl filled with something warm. "Eat up."

John stared at what looked like oatmeal. He suddenly felt ravenous. When was the last time he had eaten? He couldn't say. He couldn't remember anything past awakening in the water. He spooned a bit of the food and sampled it. A salty, fishy flavor filled his mouth instead of the creamy sweetness he'd expected, and he nearly spit it out. "What is this?"

Grizzly made a face like he was asking a silly question. "Fishmeal. What you expect?"

That didn't make him feel like eating it anymore. "Who are you?"

"Walter Andrews. But you can call me Walt."

Better than Grizzly, he supposed. John slipped on his coveralls and raincoat.

Walt handed him a miner's cap. "Let's get to work."

They left the infirmary, but not through the hatch they had entered before.

"Can't go that way now," Walt explained. "The tides up."

He led John through the infirmary and up a set of rusty stairs. About five flights they arose, passing a few other people dressed in either yellow or white raincoats. Gloom greeted them as they exited onto the roof of what John assumed was still the infirmary building. Rain pelted from a stormy night sky, but not as severe as from before. Or perhaps it was just the raincoat that helped ease the effect some.

"It's still night?" Just how long had he slept?

Walt gave him that odd look again and just laughed.

When it didn't look like he was going to get an actual response, John turned his attention to the rest of the surroundings. They were close to the same elevation as the top of the wall now. He looked toward it, and what he saw froze his breath.

On the opposite side of the hundred-foot wall, where Walt had rescued him, was now a roaring and raging sea that threatened to crest the top. Dark waves crashed like thunder against the thirty-foot thick wall, sending sea spray shooting over and into the courtyard along with the rain. The six-foot recess of the courtyard was filled with about half a foot of water sloshing with froth and foam. John looked toward the two dock cranes, and he nearly jumped with fright as he saw what now lay in between them.

Writhing next to each crane was what he could only describe as a pair of octopus-like creatures the size of an elephants. They were tethered by chain to the upturned opening of the massive transparent pipe. Most of their bodies were exposed to the air, with just a portion of their undersides touching the water that filled the pipe, their dark red skin moistened from the rain.

They weren't exactly octopi, though. More like a cross between an octopus and a squid, perhaps, with a pointed and elongated head and more than eight arms. His mind reeled, trying to comprehend if what he was seeing was actually real or not.

"What's wrong with you?" Walt backhanded him across the chest.

John snapped to his senses. "What are those things?"

"You really don't know? You are fragged, aren't you?"

John couldn't take his eyes off the massive creatures, each with at least ten arms as thick as tree trunks over thirty feet long. Their dark, mottled skin was slick and sheened in the dull glow of the green light. Their monstrous eyes were easily the size of a man's head, each with a square pupil fixed in a perpetual stare. The two octopus-things were spaced just far enough apart that it seemed to leave a five-foot gap between them, but their arms stretched toward one other…reaching.

"Cephalovores," Walt said. "We call

'em Tom and Jerry. They're the things that keep us all alive."

"How so?"

"You want to see?"

John nodded, but feared what he was about to witness next.

"They'll be starting soon. Guess we can be a few minutes late."

They waited in the rain, watching as Tom and Jerry sat idly on their tobacco pipe thrones, wading their arms in the shallow waters of the square. One of the derrick cranes suddenly roared to life with a hiss of compressed air. Thick white smoke erupted from a rusted smokestack and combined with the rain to form a kind of smog. The crane creaked with metal fatigue as it spun its massive boom toward the seawall and then lowered the tip over the water's edge.

With a sudden jerk, a net fell from the tip of the crane boom and into the rolling sea. Almost immediately the sea began to boil even fiercer, glimpses of tentacles and suction cups breaking the dark choppy waves.

The crane lifted its boom and pulled out a net easily twice the size of one of the octopus-creatures. It was strained to capacity with writhing tentacles and slippery shiny red bodies. The crane's engine groaned with the heavy load, hauling it over the wall. And then, with a quick release, it dumped the entire contents of the net before one of the cephalovores.

The shallow waters inside the square hissed and boiled as what had to be over a thousand man-sized squid fell to the ground shooting jets of water and ink vainly into the air.

One of the enormous cephalovores began tearing into the smaller version of itself with its massive tree-trunk tentacles. The splashing of water was soon joined by sickening audible squeals as the squid were shoveled up by the lightning-quick arms of the cephalovore and shoved underneath its mantle, where an enormous parrot-like beak tore into the flesh of its kin.

Black ink muddied the already dark waters as the screeches raised in a fever pitch like the cry of a thousand infants. The enormous octopus creature flashed yellow and bright orange as it gorged.

Its sibling, Jerry—John decided— flashed in reciprocal excitement, or perhaps jealously, snatching any stray squid that managed to escape its brother's grasp. But it too was soon rewarded as the second crane went into action and dumped its own load of smaller cephalopods for it to gorge upon.

"Watch the tube," Walt said, pointing to the transparent pipeline.

As soon as he did, John noticed an explosive volume of dark liquid eject itself from the underside of one of the cephalovores. It travelled swiftly down the pipe, propelled by successively quick volleys of more dark liquid. Streaks of silver fish darted up the pipe to meet the dark mass, jumping into it and swarming like flies.

"Bait fish," Walt said. "First stop on the food chain."

"Are they eating what I think they are?"

"Yup. Each of those two monsters can produce over five tons of it an hour."

"By eating their own kind?"

"Pretty much."

"So what eats the fish?"

"Bigger fish." Walt grinned. "And other things that Dr. Jefferson manages to whip up."

"Dr. Jefferson?"

"Our leader. He's who built all this. Every ounce of energy we got is thanks to those two monsters he created."

Created? "Where were they before? I didn't see them last night."

"They're stored in holding tanks below when the tide goes out."

"How often is that?"

"For a couple days each month. You ask a lot of questions."

"Sorry."

They watched Tom and Jerry in silence as the two cephalovores reveled in their cannibalistic orgy. The sight and sounds of shredding flesh and squealing death soon began to turn John's stomach. He was glad he hadn't eaten that fish slop now, else he'd probably be wearing it on his raincoat.

"They say a long time ago the sea used to be filled with all kinds of creatures," Walt said. "Just like the ones Dr. Jefferson breeds inside. Lots more, even."

John looked at him. Walt's face was somber and distant.

"So what happened?"

"Who knows?" Walt shrugged. "All we know is those days are long gone. Now all we have are these sea beasts, these monstrous squid…and the tides."

# Nether Ore

Walt led John away from the seawall, following the excretion tubes—Walt formally named them—toward a central tower that was fixed against a steep granite cliff face that was the back of the canyon.

The tower rose to about the same height as the sea wall, perhaps a bit taller, with glowing green windows marking its dull grey exterior every so often. At its base was what looked like a shantytown constructed of rusted zinc shacks, some towering three layers high. As they approached, John noticed more and more yellow raincoats, people moving in and out of the shacks, sheltering themselves from the pelting rain.

"Who lives here?" he asked.

Walt made that same dumbfounded face again. "We do. Only the scientists live in the research blocks. We miners live here."

"What do we mine?"

"Ore."

"What kind?"

Walt shrugged. "I ain't no scientist."

They traversed the shantytown, hollow

eyes from within raincoats paying them little attention as they stepped around cooking fires and makeshift sleeping places. John realized now that he should be thankful for getting that infirmary bed his first night. They joined a queue of some twenty other yellow raincoats waiting at the entrance of the tower base.

In a few minutes a loud buzzer sounded, and a gateway at the base tower lifted. A score of yellow raincoats covered in black muck exited the gate and made their way wordlessly toward the shantytown. The group John and Walt stood with trudged forward to take their place.

They squeezed into one of two elevator carts, which shook as it began its descent.

Darkness gave way to deeper darkness. Only the dull green glow of head lamps gave form to the bodies of yellowcoats pressing around him. A deep rumbling began to grow louder as they descended toward a source of brighter green light. The sound and light finally crescendoed as the elevator jerked to stop at the entrance to a relatively well-lit tunnel that led to a larger room. The door flew upward, and

John began to make his way out. A hand caught his arm.

"Not our stop," Walt said. "This is the powerhouse."

John looked past the bodies and saw a handful of the raincoats shuffling outside into the tunnel of thunderous sound and light. He caught a glimpse of its source—huge engines the size of buildings lay within a central hall. An acrid stench caught John's nose, and he gagged. "Smells like burnt fish in there."

"They run on biodiesel derived from fish oil," Walt said. "These engines make the power to run the pumps that keep the bilge water out of the city and the mines. And make all the power for everything else too. All complements of Dr. Jefferson."

"Of Tom and Jerry, you mean..."

Walt laughed. "You learn fast."

The gate closed, and the elevator began its descent again. It travelled for what seemed another ten minutes before jolting to a stop.

The gate flew upward and the entire crew exited into a swamp-like heat of utter darkness. Sweat bathed John's skin instantly as they made their way into the shaft. The walls of darkness closed in on him like the flailing arms of the sea beasts upstairs.

"You okay?" Walt grabbed his arm.

John managed a nod. "What do I do?" Walt cracked a grin, the glow of his lamp illuminating his crooked teeth. "Just stick with me."

The next twelve hours were a lesson in agony. After traveling for what seemed like half a mile following a set of railway tracks along a downward sloping horizontal shaft, they entered a slightly more expansive chamber that seemed to be the main worksite.

Pneumatic jackhammers fed by fish oil-powered compressors thundered in the darkness, adding dust, chaos, and a choking stench to the already unbearable heat. There did not seem to be much order to their activities. Or purpose, even. Everyone seemed to work randomly. Half the team of yellowcoats were on the jackhammers, while the other half scooped up debris in buckets and passed it on to a team of scientists in white raincoats, who sifted the debris before poring over it with handheld scanners.

When the whitecoats didn't appear to find what they were looking for—which seemed to happen with every bucket—they made the yellowcoats scrape up the debris and load it into a mine cart, which was then pushed by hand up the railway tracks back to the second elevator, which was used only for freight.

It was backbreaking work. John was a bucket man, as was Walt. They stopped only twice, for about half an hour each time, to eat bowls of lumpy fishmeal. This time, John devoured it—on both occasions.

By the end of the shift he was in a daze. He did not even remember anyone conversing beyond the giving of instructions. Even his stumbling walk back to the zinc shantytown with Walt was devoid of conversation.

Walt provided him a corner to sleep in within his zinc shack, which was located on the ground floor. And, after another helping of fishmeal, John drifted off to sleep.

He was in the living room again, the large sliding glass door overlooking the blue, blue sea. Karen sat cross-legged on the floor, storybook in hand. Sam and Josh sat opposite her, dressed in colorful pajamas depicting jungle animals and stars. Her voice was soothing, lovely, smooth like satin. He watched her in silence, again his family not seeming to notice him.

She was reading the children a fantastical story about a man in a boat the size of a city, filled with every animal imaginable. And then she told another story about a man being swallowed whole by a giant fish.

Finally she looked up at him and smiled. "Daddy's home."

Before they could run to greet him, his dream faded yet again.

Time passed, measured only by shifts in the mine and the short sleeps he got in the rain-soaked shantytown in the corner of Walt's zinc shack. Each day, John kept hoping his memory would return, that he'd somehow recall where he was from and how he had come to this place—perhaps even remember a way home. But other than in his dreams, nothing ever came. After a while he gave up on the possibility.

Perhaps his mind was damaged just like they all said.

The toil in the mines seemed endless. Each shift they pursued the elusive ore that no one seemed able to identify, save the whitecoats who oversaw their work. Every so often, one of them would announce a discovery. And then a clinical ceremony would be performed, in which the usually pebble-sized piece of rock would be secured in a bottle of liquid.

John estimated that happened once maybe every ten of his shifts. Probably it happened about that often in the alternate shifts too.

When it did happen, their crew would receive an extra ration of fish oil diesel for "doing a good job." They'd then draw straws, and the man with the short straw would have to go topside with a hook and gaff and try and snatch a young squid from the ravenous beaks of Tom and Jerry. It seemed the only source of entertainment for the city. Especially for the whitecoats, who stood on their roofs to see if the lone soul would end up predator or prey. It was a risky business, but seemed safe enough when done right. Usually a stray squid would wonder far enough away from the cephalovores for the man to snatch it up with ease.

Then they would gut the monster, stick it on a rusty pole, and hang it over a flaming barrel of fish oil diesel. When cooked, the creature's meat tasted little better than the fishmeal. But its meaty texture was a welcome change, and every now and then a bit of char would add flavor that bordered on appetizing.

But the best part of all were the stories.

Around the stench of burning fish oil and huddled within the rain free refuge of their zinc shacks, they would tell stories of the old days. Apparently there had been a time when there was light in the sky for as long as a shift, and when darkness lasted only a shift as well—day and night. Animals in abundance, trees. Fish of every kind swam in the sea. And people could swim in the sea as well, without being burned by caustic water or devoured in seconds by the same creatures they now feasted upon.

It was odd in a sense. They spoke of things John had never recalled seeing with his own eyes. Yet somehow he knew what they were just by name. Brain-damaged, they told him he was. His memories were fragmented. Fragged.

"I think I have a wife," he told them once. "I see her and my two children in my dreams."

None of them seemed particularly surprised—or even interested, for that matter.

"It happens," Walt said. "The memories come back sometimes. But that's all they are. Whoever she is…was…she's long gone now. Just like everything else."

The shifts continued—the aching of muscles and the swelter of heat and the stink of fish oil within the green gloom of the mine's deep shafts. John learned the routine. He rotated between the jackhammers and the shoveling, but his favorite activity was removing the debris via the rail cart.

Not that it was any easier. In fact, it was the most arduous job to be had. But it did allow a brief respite to the surface. In time, they let him do it nearly every shift. He'd notice things on his trips, like how many whitecoats would stop to get off at the power house throughout the day. One time he stopped the freight elevator at the powerhouse level and then sat quietly and just watched. He saw at least three elevator loads of whitecoats enter from the adjacent personnel shaft. Were so many scientists needed to run the powerhouse?

Sometimes he thought about risking a venture into the brightly lit shaft to see those huge engines for himself. But the whitecoats in the mines kept time, and being late would mean he would be relegated to more menial duties.

While the powerhouse was a curiosity, it could not compare with the faint glimpse of the outdoors he got every few hours… even if it was only of a perpetual rainy night sky.

True escape came with sleep—and in his dreams. He didn't dream every night, but when he did, he tried to make it last as long as possible. He especially enjoyed when Karen told the children stories. It seemed his dreams would end the moment his family noticed him, so he would stay quiet and listen as long as possible.

It was the same book each night. Stories of kingdoms long past, of people with long and complicated names. Of a being called God that was the creator of everything. About a man named Christ Jesus, who was supposed to save the entire world from some terrible destruction. The stories went on and on. But each time, as soon as they saw him, their faces would light up, and then his dream would end.

"I drew the short straw."

Walt frowned as he told John. He then looked at him with pleading eyes. "Want to come with me?"

John nodded. It was only fair. "I was the one who found the ore, after all."

They left the confines of the mine and walked through the shantytown together. John carried the ten-foot-long gaff fashioned with a rusty barbed hook the size of his head. The rain was heavy, driven by a strong wind.

By the time they made it to the square, it looked as if a full-blown squall had set in. Waves twenty feet high crested the top of the sea wall, dumping seawater and squid into the square nearly as fast as the two dock cranes feeding Tom and Jerry.

"Not a good day for this," Walt said as

he looked over the expanse that lay between the concrete-block buildings the whitecoats called home.

There had to be four feet of water sloshing about the recess, barely two feet from the edge where it would then spill toward their shantytown and the mine. John thought about how hard those pumps and engines had to be running to keep the water level from rising farther within the square. The amount of fish oil diesel they had to be burning. That brought him back to the excretion tubes, the transparent thrones of Tom and Jerry, where they sat and gorged and provided the raw fuel for their existence.

The cephalovores seemed particularly stimulated, flashing bright orange and red as they tore into their smaller cousins and filled the excretion tubes with a steady stream of dark fodder.

"Let me do it," John said.

Walt looked at him, seeming suddenly very old and very frail. How he endured the mines each shift, John still did not know.

"No, no..." Walt shook his head and snatched the gaff from him. "My luck, my chore. Just make sure I don't fall in."

# Nether Ore

John trailed Walt as he walked along the recess edge, getting a bit closer to the feeding frenzy ahead. The sight up close made John's stomach turn. Not only were Tom and Jerry eating the smaller squid, but the squid were mindlessly attacking and eating each other as well—a last chance to gorge before being gorged upon.

John looked up and saw the usual crowd of whitecoats gathered on their rooftops to watch the show. Perhaps a bit more than normal, actually.

"Here looks good," Walt said, stopping at the corner closest to the wall. "We'll wait for the next net-full and hopefully catch us a fresh one."

It didn't take long. Soon the crane delivered its payload and restocked the feeding frenzy anew. The snapping of beaks and the squeal of death filled the air with a sickening din. John took hold of the back of Walt's raincoat as he leaned over the recess edge and began fishing with his gaff.

Minutes went by. They waited for one of the squid to stray far enough from the center to give them a chance at a catch. The rain and breaking waves crashed over them, proving a perpetual deluge from above.

Walt jerked back on the pole and his hook jabbed into a nice young squid about the size of a man's leg. Walt let out a shout of victory and laughed as he hauled in his catch. "All in the wrist," he said with a grin. Suddenly a larger squid, perhaps sensing the distress of its sibling, latched around the head of the gaff and began devouring the smaller cephalopod. The pole jerked Walt's arms back and forth like a piston on a crank.

"Let go!" John cried.

"I got it! I got—"

A thunderous wave crashed overhead, and all at once Walt lost his footing and went skidding into the foaming water, pulled by the gaff.

"Walt!"

John leapt into the dark waves and managed to snatch the collar of Walt's raincoat. The frigid water doused his coveralls and slowly started to burn. Walt had let go of the gaff. The pole whipped back and forth by whatever was still caught on its hook. But something was still pulling Walt.

"My leg!" he cried. "It's got my leg."

John reached into the water and felt

the slimy skin of a squid latched onto Walt's thigh. Adrenaline surged as John made a fist and tried to beat it off him, but the water absorbed the power of his blows. He resorted to gripping the flesh and digging into it with his fingernails. He felt it tugging loose.

And then a tentacle latched itself around his forearm. Pain like fire shot through his arm as what felt like a million razors cut into his flesh. He gritted his teeth and increased the grip on the thing, hoping it was only one of them.

Walt began shouting curses in screams of rage, which quickly devolved into just screams.

John glanced up and saw they had been dragged nearly halfway toward the center of the square. One monstrous eye of Tom, or Jerry, whichever one it was, loomed above them. It was impossible to tell if it had noticed them or not with its static square pupil stare. But John wasn't going to wait around to find out. They were already close enough for one of its giant arms to reach them.

John summoned his strength and dug into the squid with a cry of desperation. Finally his fingers broke skin. His hand dug into the rubbery flesh, and almost immediately the tentacle tore away from his forearm, and the creature jetted away. John half-ran, half-swam toward the recess edge, hauling Walt with one arm around his chest.

Walt wasn't screaming anymore, and that made John swim even faster.

He felt something latch around his own legs, and he cried out, kicking at it with sheer defiance. Whatever it was decided he wasn't worth the battle and, thankfully, jetted away.

Adrenaline and panic fueled his muscles, and he all but flew across the water, hauling the full weight of Walt as easily as if he were a child. He reached the edge and tossed Walt onto the concrete and then hauled himself out.

Instantly the exertion of what he had just done set in, and he collapsed to his knees. His lungs rasped for breath like he'd just run a marathon. After a few seconds of recuperation he looked to Walt—and suddenly understood why it had been so easy to drag him in.

There was nothing of Walt from the thighs down. What was left of his legs were now a bleeding mess of torn muscle and veins.

"*Walt!*"

Miraculously there was a response. "I...I messed up."

"Someone help!" John cried out.

He looked to the concrete roofs and saw that the whitecoats hadn't moved from their perches. They all stood there gawking, not even a flutter of activity or panic in reaction to what they had seen. Then slowly they began to filter back from the edges of the rooftops and into their homes.

John couldn't believe their indifference. No, it far worse than that. It was more like...disappointment.

Anger filled his blood with fire hotter than the wound burning his arm. "He's still alive! Someone help him, please!"

"It's okay," Walt said softly. "It was getting around to my time anyway."

"You're going to make it, Walt." John tore off his raincoat and used each arm to make tourniquet wraps for Walt's legs. He twisted the rubbery material until he was certain it was tight enough to not allow further blood loss.

Walt was in shock and in a mammoth amount of pain, but he seemed to calm some and even spoke again. "For what it's worth, John…I thank you."

The rain and seawater started to irritate his skin, the stinging growing nearly unbearable. But he dared not leave Walt to seek relief. "Just relax. We'll—"

"What do you think you're doing?"

John turned around and saw a whitecoat and about a half-dozen yellowcoats standing over them.

"You risk two bodies being lost instead of just one?" the whitecoat asked.

John looked up under the whitecoat's hood and recognized the face—gaunt with wispy combed-over hair and steely blue eyes. It was the same scientist he had seen the night he was found. "He's hurt," John said, "but I think if we can get him to the infir—"

"He's too badly injured," Blue Eyes said. "Toss him back in."

"What?"

"Remove his coat first."

Before John could raise a voice of protest, the six yellowcoats pushed him aside.

Walt screamed as four of them lifted him off the ground and began to swing him back and forth. "No, please! No!"

"Walt!"

The yellowcoats tossed Walt high into the air. He released a shrill cry that was silenced as he splashed down somewhere near the middle of the square.

The water immediately boiled with flashing bodies, tentacles, ink, and blood. Then the entire area erupted as a giant arm scooped up the frenzy and dragged it toward the giant beak of either Tom or Jerry.

For the briefest moment, John saw a glimpse of Walt's face. Whether he was already dead or not, John didn't know, but he prayed that he was when he saw the entire mass of writhing bodies stuffed under the giant mantle of the cephalovore.

"That should spice up the fish meal," the whitecoat said with a laugh.

Rage filled him, and without thinking John was on his feet and charging the whitecoat.

He never reached him. Six pairs of hands grabbed him all at once and pinned him to the ground. The whitecoat stepped over him and then removed his hood, his blue eyes scanning him. "I remember you. You're that reinstate they supposedly found beyond the wall last tide. I should probably have you fed back to the—"

"Everything all right, Dr. Morris?"

The voice was deep and authoritative, and instantly Blue Eyes straightened himself. "Yes, Dr. Jefferson. Everything is fine."

Jefferson. The leader. The creator of all these horrors. John strained his neck to get a look at the whitecoat now joining the blue-eyed Dr. Morris. He was a bit shorter and had a thick greying beard.

"Just some miner that's forgotten it's pointless to save someone from the arms of a cephalovore, sir."

Jefferson studied him. "I see. Perhaps I should see to having him reinstated."

There was that word again.

"No, no," Dr. Morris said. "He's still young." The blue-eyed devil gave him a grin. "Let him work instead."

Jefferson worked his jaw side to side. "Very well."

That night no dreams came. Only the nightmares of losing his friend.

Work seemed much harder in the mines in the days that followed. The wounds on his arm healed, but the wounds inside festered with resentment and despair.

The shifts wore on. John no longer cared to travel to the surface with the mine cart duty. He stayed within the bowels of the mine—hammering, shoveling. Mindless work to keep his thoughts from focusing on the horrors of this place. The crew didn't seem to care that Walt was gone. They didn't even speak of him, or to each other, for that matter. When they eventually did speak, it was about six days later when someone found another piece of ore.

"Barbeque time," one of the whitecoats said as he analyzed the nugget of rock with his handheld device. "Hope you fellas catch a big one."

Almost immediately the work crew stopped, and someone produced the straws to draw from.

John could barely believe it. He watched as they eagerly drew lots, smiles emerging as they savored what was soon to come.

"You really want to try gaffing another squid after what happened to Walt?"

The crew looked up at him blankly, some remorsefully—shamefully.

Finally one of them spoke. "But it's...
What else would we do with it?"

What would they do with what? John
supposed they meant the fish oil.

"Forget him," someone blurted from
the dark. "Draw the straws."

"Why? So we can burn another
squid?" John shouted at them. "Eat its
flesh the way they seek to devour ours?
And then what? Waste away in this mine,
searching for some ore that only these
whitecoats seem to care about, just so we
can do again? And again? And again? Is
that all we exist for?"

"Hey!" one of the whitecoats said.
"Settle down now."

John leveled his eyes at the whitecoat
who had spoken. "They give us a chance
to risk our lives and then view it as sport.
Tell us the truth, whitecoat. What's the real
reason we're down here? What are we
mining for?"

"I told you to settle down!"

"Or what?" John's anger flared and
filled his veins with adrenaline and hate.
He balled his fists and stomped toward the
group of three whitecoats. "Will you feed
me to the cephalovores, the same way you
did Walt?"

# Nether Ore

"What's wrong with him?" The whitecoat retreated a bit and turned to one of his colleagues. "Better report this to Dr. —"

"Please, no!" One of the yellowcoats jumped up and stood in between John and the scientist. "Don't listen to him. He's just fragged. He doesn't have memory of anything. Bad reinstatement."

That stupid word again.

"Hold him then," the whitecoat said. "I'll check."

Before John could protest, his work crew seized him, pinning his arms behind his back.

The whitecoat in charge ran the sickly green light of his scanner over John's forehead. He made a face and turned to one of his colleagues. "Not getting a reading. Let me borrow yours."

The two whitecoats swapped instruments, and the test was repeated. "Still nothing. Must be some serious degradation. Let me check if there's some physical damage. Get me the x-ray."

One of his lackeys handed him a new device, and he leveled it with John's head, studying the scope on the other side for a good minute or two. Then suddenly he stopped and backed up, pressing into the other whitecoats.

"By Jefferson," he said. "This man is alive."

Every hand released him.

What had he just said?

"No!" the whitecoat cried. "Keep hold of him! He's more precious than a thousand pieces of ore!"

That was all the verification John needed to solidify his decision to flee.

He spun about and took off up the mineshaft toward the elevators. He still wasn't sure what had happened. He sprinted through the darkness, the dim glow of his headlamp barely able to illuminate enough for him to avoid running into the jagged walls of the shaft. He could hear the commotion of a pursuit forming behind him, but he had adrenalin on his side. He pressed on and eventually reached the elevator shaft.

Fortunately, only the freight elevator was present. He could take it, and they would have to wait for the personnel elevator to arrive before they could follow him. He jumped inside, slammed closed the gate, and cranked the lever skyward. It rose, and in the lull of his ascent he fought to bring his breathing back under control.

It also gave him time to think.

What had that whitecoat meant?

He wasn't certain, but being more valuable than ore probably wasn't a good status to obtain in this place. It might keep him out of the cephalovore pit, but it might put him into some other kind of danger. Something that involved the scientists opening up his brain or the like.

He thought about his escape. Where exactly would he go? Where could he go? The place was like a prison. There was only the mine, the shantytown, and the seawall. Nothing beyond.

Then he saw the light from the powerhouse shaft.

They would most likely assume he would flee to the surface. Ducking into the powerhouse would at least buy him some more time to think. He stopped the elevator and exited into the strong green glow and the thunderous din of the biodiesel engines.

Heat similar to that in the mines greeted him as he traveled down the shaft, which opened into a cavern half the size of the square. The sound seemed magnified, and he had to hold his hands over his ears so not to go mad from the noise. He hustled across the floor, which was concrete and covered in oil stains. The reek of burnt fish oil was nearly unbearable, a hundred times worse than what was put out by their little compressors down in the mines.

He spotted a few yellowcoats walking around the engines, but they didn't seem to notice him. Massive metal pipes hung along the walls and ceiling, painted in various colors according to some kind of identification scheme. There were labels too—Fuel Oil, Lube Oil, Exhaust Flue, Intake Air. He followed the fuel oil lines to the back of the cavern and saw a control booth manned by two whitecoats. Next to it was a corridor entrance marked: NO ENTRY.

Was that where all the whitecoats went each day?

John hid behind one of the engines, wondering if he should just go back to the elevator and take his chances on the surface. Then his heart leapt as he saw one of the whitecoats leave the booth and head in his direction.

He pressed himself against the side of the engine casing, its heat quickly burning through his raincoat and warming his back like an iron. He risked another glance. Sure enough, the whitecoat was making a beeline straight for him.

Had he been spotted?

John backed up a little. Perhaps there was a place he could hide. He looked up at the mammoth engines. There was a walkway above him and some pipework he could perhaps squeeze behind. He started toward it when suddenly something brushed past him.

The whitecoat.

He walked right past, oblivious. Had he maybe taken him for one of the power plant operators? Yellow raincoats all looked the same, after all.

But then...so did white ones.

John ignored his rational senses and instead snuck up behind the whitecoat. He tapped him on the shoulder. The man felt that. He stopped and turned around. And John slammed a fist into his jaw.

The whitecoat spun and collapsed in a heap, much to John's relief and surprise. John wasted no time in swapping coats with the man. He hid him on the upper platform among the pipes and headed across the open floor to the NO ENTRY corridor.

John made a point to walk casually, like it was a daily routine. He slipped past the whitecoat in the booth, who seemed busy tending to gauges. Finally, he was through and into the forbidden corridor.

John entered a second chamber similar in size to the first. It was more dimly lit, which he was thankful for, but it was also about a hundred times more cluttered. All manner of tanks and equipment filled the space from ceiling to floor. He spotted a stray whitecoat here and there, but they seemed so absorbed in whatever they were doing that he didn't feel threatened by them at all, especially when wearing one of their coats.

As he let his breath calm, he studied the room in more detail. For all its clutter there was definitely order. Every pipe and piece of equipment was labeled. The first thing he noticed were the two massive transparent tubes running along the ceiling, labeled Ex 1 and Ex 2. They dumped into a tank at the front of the room where an aquarium of small fish were feasting upon the influx of fodder. From there, the muddy water left via two pipes, one labeled "Diesel Processing" and the other "Aquaculture."

The fish oil line went through several pieces of complicated looking equipment, but the termination was a massive storage tank that had pipes leading back to the diesel generators. He followed the Aquaculture line and saw tank after tank of increasingly large fish. At the end, they were netted out and put through a device that was labeled Fishmeal Processor. That device had a further series of pipes that were labeled with names like Food Storage and Fertilizer. But one label caught his attention immediately: "Reinstatement Chamber."

John checked for other whitecoats before tracing the ten-inch diameter line and seeing where it would lead. He followed it, walking up a series of metal steps and along a walkway that led out the room and into another corridor.

It emptied into a room that held the brightest light John had ever seen since coming to this place. He was up on a suspended walkway overlooking a room lit by more than a hundred lamps hung from the ceiling next to him. What he saw below staggered his mind.

Rows of green vegetation, grasses, and

even trees sprung from soil as black as charcoal. The sweet aroma of flowers triggered memories of his dreams—his wife and children reading stories by the light of the sun.

He wanted to stay to admire the sight, but he kept moving for fear that one of the whitecoats milling about below would suddenly look up and take note of him. He pressed on, following the tube through yet another short corridor.

The next room he entered was again the same size, but ice cold. Artificial cooling poured from large vents hung from the ceiling. It was a welcome change to the humidity and heat. He looked below and saw what looked like a miniature city comprised of large black metal cabinets affixed with what had to be hundreds upon hundreds of tiny glass bulbs.

Toward the back of the room, a team of whitecoats sat at desks. Before them were large circular screens covered in pale green writing. They clacked at controls constantly, staring at the screens as numbers and letters flashed quickly by.

He crossed through into an adjoining room, which was both cool and dark. He followed the fishmeal pipe until it ended at the top of a large rectangular tank. From the tank bottom came a network of smaller pipes that spread out in a matrix and then hung down as tubes from the ceiling. John followed one of the tubes into the darkness and then leaned over the catwalk and adjusted his miner's lamp to get a better view of what lay below.

Tethered to the end of the tube was a dead body suspended by chains.

John jerked back in horror. Sweat greased his palms and his heart thundered in his ears. Reluctantly he followed another tube and saw yet another dead body. His flesh crawled and his stomach felt sick. The entire room was filled with dead people. Naked bodies hanging from the ceiling like animals to be slaughtered.

He shouldn't be seeing this. What would they do to him if they found him here? He had to get out of this place.

John spun, and immediately something struck him hard in the face. He fell backward, and his vision blurred with tears and stars. His back slammed onto the catwalk floor, and the impact stole his breath.

When his vision cleared, he saw a group of whitecoats standing over him.

One he recognized instantly as Dr. Morris. He brandished a club…and a self-satisfied grin. Next to him was Jefferson.

"Sneaky," Morris said. "I should have been more intuitive about you. Our prized jewel hiding right beneath our noses."

"What are you going to do to me?"

"Teach you some manners, perhaps."

"Bring him to me," Jefferson said. "I want to speak with him." He turned and disappeared into the darkness.

Morris waited, perhaps deliberately, until Jefferson was out of earshot and then raised his club again. John remembered two or three hits to his head before finally blacking out.

Sunshine gleamed through the open sliding glass door, the blue sea horizon beyond it.

John could smell the sweet scent of sea air on the breeze. Sam and Josh were playing together on living room floor, but they looked different, older. They were bickering over a toy airplane. Then he saw a third child, a girl, not yet a toddler, seated on her chubby brown haunches—

soundlessly enthralled by the impromptu pantomime of her older brothers.

"Be careful around Sophie," Karen called from down the hall.

Karen... Oh, how he longed to see her again—at least just one more time. She appeared. Her locks had been cut shorter. She looked more mature and a bit heavier around the midsection, but she still looked every bit as beautiful as he remembered.

She looked surprised to see him, startled almost. But she smiled. "You've been gone a long time."

As always he couldn't speak, but he tried anyhow. Please let me stay!

"Sophie, come see your daddy." Karen reached down for the little girl, and the child's pumpkin face lit up with a toothless smile. The boys cried out with excitement in unison.

And, like always, his dream came to an end.

Perhaps for the last time.

John awoke to find himself seated in a chair. He stirred so abruptly he nearly fell out of it. He braced himself by catching hold of a metal table that was in front of him.

He became aware of how bright everything was. It took a moment for his eyes to adjust, but slowly he realized he was in the infirmary or someplace like it. The room had several medical beds and strange sterile-looking pieces of equipment made of shiny steel. The place stunk of ammonia.

Seated across from him at the end of the table was Dr. Jefferson. His raincoat hood had been removed, revealing a bald and weathered head, wrinkled eyes, and a full grey beard. Next to him was Dr. Morris, sans hood as well. He scowled smugly, and his comb-over was revealed in full.

Then John saw something he hadn't noticed. Before him was a dinner plate— with a slab of grilled meat, string beans, and a potato on it. It almost didn't look real.

"I figured we owed you a decent meal after all we've put you through," Jefferson said. "Please go ahead. You must be starving for something other than fishmeal."

John eyed the silver cutlery next to the

plate, and his stomach growled in response. His body yearned for the flavors of food he somehow knew, yet couldn't recall ever experiencing. Then he thought about the dead bodies he had seen, and somehow the slab of meat didn't look appetizing anymore.

He shoved the plate away.

"Not hungry?" Morris smiled at him.

"Good. Then we can begin. Let's start with how you got here."

"Please..." Jefferson touched Morris's forearm. "I'm sure he has more questions for us than we do for him. Your name is John, correct?"

He nodded.

"I'm sure you wish to know what this place is."

"Yes," he said. "As a start."

"We don't have a name for it," Jefferson said. "There is no need. As far as we know, this is the only place still left in existence."

That didn't strike him as very reassuring.

"We still don't know for certain how things came to be this way or exactly how long ago it all happened. What we do know is that it's been centuries since we've seen the sun. Some believe it's the result of a cataclysmic war. Others hypothesize that the world has stopped spinning, or now spins very slowly, creating a perpetual day and night. I myself believe it to be something far more dire, but I'll come to that. My name is Dr. Jefferson. I am the leader of this community. And this is Dr. Morris my second in command."

"I caught your names earlier, thanks." John wondered how long this mock civility would last and when the club would come back out. "I want to know what you plan to do with me."

"Nothing," Jefferson said. "But I'm sure you must have many more questions for us. Please do ask them."

Guess he had nothing to lose. "What does this place do? What's this ore we mine? And why am I worth more than a thousand pieces of it?"

"All excellent questions," Jefferson said. "What we do is simple: We survive. That's it. As for the ore that you mine, it is on the plate before you."

John looked down at the food and wondered if he were joking or mad.

"The ecosystem of this world has collapsed. Cephalopods were the only things to survive—and they did that only by constantly breeding and feeding upon themselves. We mine the earth for remnants of the past, stray genes of life. So that we may clone it, and bring it back from extinction."

"So this food…"

"All came from a fragment of DNA preserved in a rock that was mined from below. Perhaps you recovered this bit yourself. We've mined for hundreds of years and still have only ever found a handful of complete DNA chains to reproduce a small number of species."

He thought of the greenhouse room he'd passed through. "Why do you feed the miners fishmeal when you have food like this?"

"It's more efficient," Morris said. "Real food takes time and energy to grow. We can't waste it on the labor force."

"But it's good enough to waste on the whitecoats?"

"On some," he said.

"What other questions do you have?" Jefferson asked.

John ignored his contempt for Morris and focused on the questions he needed answers to. He could come up with only one. "What is reinstatement?"

Jefferson glanced over to Morris before looking back to him. "I think I need to show you something for you to understand fully," Jefferson said. "Please come with me."

They left the infirmary and descended a flight of stairs. Instantly John recognized that they were entering the climate controlled room with the large black cabinets and flashing screens he had seen before. The whitecoats at the screens barely acknowledged their presence as Jefferson led them between the metal cabinets. John marveled at the row upon row of tiny bulbs that flickered on and off with pale green light. Finally Jefferson stopped, and Morris stopped next him.

"I wish to tell you a secret," Jefferson said. "Every person in this facility is dead." Adrenalin pounded his heart with fright.

"Everyone…is…" John couldn't make his mouth form any more words.

"Dead," Jefferson said. "Yes. All except you."

That sent further chills up his spine.

He took an involuntary step backward.

"Please let me explain," Jefferson said. "In the beginning, when we first established this place, there were hundreds of us. But we grew sterile. Since we couldn't conceive, we turned to cloning to replenish our numbers. I've cloned many things, John: plants, animals, bacteria. All become healthy replicas of the original. But when we tried to clone a human, it would never wake."

"What do you mean?"

"You saw the room next door, yes? With the bodies."

His skin crawled at just the thought of it, but he managed a nod.

"Technically those bodies you saw are alive. There is nothing physiologically wrong with them. But they never gain consciousness. They never live. They never wake."

"But we overcame the problem," Morris said. "Or rather, I did. With this..." He raised his hands to the cabinets around them.

"We call it the memory bank," Jefferson said. "What you see are electronic machines that can process and store the memory and thoughts of a human being. Each tube you see is equivalent to five years of recorded life. We implanted ourselves with these devices to store our memories. Then when we died we transplanted them into our clones, so they would come to life with our thoughts and memories intact. We call the process reinstatement."

"Eventually we found it more efficient to store the memories externally and operate the bodies remotely with a simple transmitter," Morris said. "Maintaining these memories requires constant electrical power. Over half the power that we produce is used to run either the circuits or the cooling system for it."

John could barely process what he was hearing. A machine that stored memories? Clones that could be implanted with a lifetime of thoughts? Was this the reason they'd called him fragmented, why he couldn't remember anything yet knew things he had never experienced before?

"The two men you see before you are merely husks," Jefferson said, patting his sternum. "Our true selves are here within the machine." He pointed to two separate panels, and John saw they were indeed labeled Jefferson and Morris. Jefferson's panel took up three entire cabinets and had well over a hundred glass bulbs. Morris's assembly was about half that size. John did the math. "You mean you've actually lived for this long?"

"My memories have," Jefferson said. "Close to a thousand years."

"What about the others? Is everyone like this?"

"We can't spare this much storage space for everyone," Morris said. "Especially when we needed labor for the mines. Like I said, memory consumes power, and the machines require constant cooling. The miners you see are merely memory fragment copies. We give them just enough to let them know who they are and their station in life." He pointed to another panel. "See here. What was that friend of yours called again? The one who went fishing?"

Anger prickled beneath his skin. "His name was Walt. Walt Andrews."

Morris paced a few cabinets, then he bent down and pointed toward some tubes. "Here he is. Alive and kicking yet again."

John stooped and saw two tiny bulbs that were cordoned off with white tape and labeled W. Andrews. There were at least twenty such names marked off like that. "I don't believe you."

"I could bring him here if you like," Morris said. "But unfortunately he wouldn't remember you. As you can see, we can only spare ten years of memory for him. Anything gained during his lifetime is lost on reinstatement."

John felt like he might pass out. Surely none of this was real. "So you mean he's alive again, but just a copy of himself?"

"A younger version, if you will," Jefferson said. "With the amount of labor we require for the mines, and the memory requirements for our technical staff—the whitecoats, as you call them—there is little room to spare. It's the only way we can afford to do things here."

"It's why we don't waste resources on them either." Morris straightened and folded his hands behind his back. "They live and work and die, and then they come back brand new to do it all over again. The men you worked with have all lived a hundred lifetimes, over and over. To treat one as special makes no sense. They're no different than squid, really."

Anger and sickness crept into his

stomach as he stared at the two twinkling lights that were his friend. He didn't want to believe it. Couldn't believe it. "Just like squid? So who decided who gets to be a squid or not? Who decides who has the right to live on or simply start again?"

"I do," Morris said almost proudly, arrogantly. "As of now, only Jefferson and I have memory growth. Everyone else is curtailed. Even the other scientists you see."

"But it can't go on forever," Jefferson said. "Every five years we two consume more and more space on the board. We must be reborn with all our memories, you see, or we can never progress. So to preserve our knowledge, the memory of others must be sacrificed in turn. That's why finding you is so important, John."

This was wrong. All so very wrong. "But I don't..." He just stared at the two bulbs.

"There is one last thing I must show you," Jefferson said. "Please follow me."

They left the memory bank area and entered the room he dreaded the most— the reinstatement chamber. Only this time he entered from below, not above. Hanging all around them were the cloned corpses of a hundred dead people—or not dead, whichever was truly the case. Jefferson strode between them like they were coats on a rack and headed toward a sickly green light at the center of the room. As they got closer John saw it shining down on a podium, and upon it was an open book.

"I came across this in the mines about two hundred years ago," Jefferson said. "And it entirely changed my thinking about what has truly happened to this world and what we now must do."

John edged closer, saw fine print on yellowed paper.

"It's a book about the God of all creation. The true architect of life—the life that we now dig to find scraps of and clumsily piece back together. This book foretells an end of days when those loyal to a divine being known as Christ Jesus will be saved, and the rest will be left behind to be damned. I fear that that day may have already come to pass."

Chills raked his skin. He knew of the story. It seemed impossible, but... "I know this book," he said. "And this tale."

Jefferson lifted his gaze, eyes filled with shock. Then his eyes softened with laugher and even tears. "That confirms it then…"

"Confirms what?"

"That you truly are the sign from God that I have prayed for."

John swallowed the dry lump in his throat.

"You, John, are the first living soul to exist for over a thousand years. You have no device controlling your body like the puppets we've been reduced to. The God of all creation has breathed into you His Spirit, and you have become a living soul! I had long believed that God had forsaken us. But I prayed for a sign of redemption. And behold, here you are. A living soul who already knows the words of God. This is confirmation!"

"It confirms nothing!" Morris said hostilely. "Where did you learn of this book? Did you peek at it earlier while you were in here?"

"No… I saw it in my dreams."

"Your… Your dreams?"

"Yes. I dreamt I had a wife and she would read stories from this book to our children."

"Sounds like memories to me." Morris looked to Jefferson. "We need to discover where he came from. I've always said there was a strong probability of people still existing somewhere beyond the sea, on the light side of the world where the sun still shines. He was found outside the sea wall. Clearly he has simply lost his memory. Perhaps he was washed overboard and swept in by the tide. If he has children, his DNA is still pure."

"That's all just speculation."

"And your theory is not?" Morris breathed heavily, his nostrils flaring. "The degradation of our samples is why we can't make healthy clones. Not some curse from your superstitious God! You need to start thinking like a scientist and clone him to —"

"No!" Jefferson shouted. "We cannot. God has sent him as a sign and a final test. We must resist the temptation to defile His creation for our selfish gain."

"You've gone mad, Jefferson!" Morris shouted. "This is our chance to repopulate our species! And if he regains his memory, he could lead us back to true civilization!"

"No… God has sent him for a purpose." Jefferson approached John and took hold of his arm. "Please…tell me, John. What is the message that God has sent with you? What is it we must do to atone for our sins? Must we destroy this abomination of life that we have created? Is that why you have come?"

"You stupid old fool!"

Jefferson's head jarred to the side with a sickening crack.

John jerked back in shock. Morris was standing over him, brandishing his club now slick with his colleague's blood. Before John could even react, Morris sent two more sickening blows to Jefferson's already battered skull.

He leered over the body. "I've waited centuries to do that."

John didn't waste a moment. He spun and ran. He sprinted blindly in the dark and slammed into one of the bodies. It swung back and it hit him, heavy and sickly cold. It took all his might not to cry out in morbid disgust at just the feel of it.

"There's nowhere to run, John!" Morris was not far behind him. "Or are you going to take your chances with the squid?"

For a split second he thought about turning and standing his ground, but no way could he defend himself in this dark, especially with Morris having a weapon.

He ran toward the light of the memory bank room and burst into the cooled air. Two whitecoats immediately headed toward him shouting for him to stop.

How had Morris alerted them so quickly? One glance at the banks of electronic bulbs, and it made sense. He wouldn't be surprised if Morris had some means of contacting, if not controlling, all of his drones remotely. John easily side-stepped the two whitecoats and ran down one of the aisleways between bulb-filled cabinets.

He heard Morris's voice shouting orders close behind. John spun about and saw him literally running down the aisle at him. John ducked around the corner of a cabinet and began scanning the rows of bulbs as fast as he could. *Please...please.*

Finally he saw what he was looking for.

Just as Morris rounded the corner John kicked at the panel of bulbs. Sparks and glass shattered, raining debris on the concrete floor. He heard Morris cry out, which encouraged him to give the cabinet —the cabinet labeled "Morris"—another healthy kick.

He looked back and was shocked to see Morris still standing. His cry had not been a cry at all, but a laugh. "Very clever, John. But a good investor always knows how to hedge his bets. I relocated my memory from that area centuries ago. Sad to say, but I couldn't put it past that old fool Jefferson trying something foolish like unplugging us all."

Time to run. That was his only hope.

John sprinted again. How could he stop this monster now?

He flew through the sweltering heat of the greenhouse garden and then through the maze of equipment in the main processing room. He could hear Morris mustering up more and more lackeys behind him. Finally John entered the well-lit powerhouse and its din. He stopped dead in his tracks when he saw what was there.

What had to be the entire mining force had formed a half circle around the corridor exit and the small control booth next to it. A small part of him hoped it was some kind of rebellion or uprising, but the mining tools they wielded were clearly meant to be used on him.

"I'm sorry you had to resort to all that." Morris's voice came from behind.

John turned about and saw Morris

entering the powerhouse with at least twenty whitecoats behind him. "Now, I'm a fair man, John. So I propose we let bygones be bygones and start over. Let's start communicating as civil human beings, yes?"

Morris stopped a few feet from him and slipped his club into his raincoat. "To tell you the truth," he said, "I truly don't care where you actually come from, John. In fact I don't care if there are a billion people living on the other side of this planet. My reality is here. But I do need your help to make it better."

"My help?"

"Trust me—I don't actually need your help," he said. "I could just take what I need from you. But it would be easier and more beneficial if you gave it."

"Gave what?"

"Your assistance in repopulating this place," he said, "with real people."

He couldn't imagine what that would mean.

"Don't believe a word that old fool was saying about souls and God. It's all within the DNA why our clones have failed. Our samples have degraded. But once I extract your fresh DNA, I will create an entire population of your descendants. And I could make it pleasurable for you as well. How many wives would you like to start out with? Ten? Twenty perhaps? All would be the finest of pedigree, of course. It'd actually be nice to have some women about here again. We stopped making them, you see. No point to it and plus they used to cause some nasty sexual tension problems with the men." He cracked a grin. "But you would be special. You could rule here as a king among men. I'd take care of the day-to–day, and you could stay busy keeping your wives barefoot and pregnant or occupy your time with eating, sleeping, or whatever leisure pursuit you'd like."

"Sounds splendid." John smirked. "And how do you benefit from all this? You'll still be tied to that stupid machine no matter how many 'real' people you make."

"Indeed," he said. "But with real people I could do away with most of these facsimiles and have the memory bank room I require to expand my longevity for generations to come. The people you spawn will need a leader after you grow old and pass away. And I shall be that leader for them. An immortal, all-knowing, all-creating leader. I shall be their god, if you like."

The thought sickened him. "No way will I help you do anything."

"Then it's the hard way for you." Morris pulled his club from his coat.

"Your DNA will work no matter—"

"I'm shocked, Morris."

John froze and searched the whitecoats for who had spoken. Morris paused and looked over his shoulder toward the voice as well.

Behind him, within the control booth was a whitecoat whose face John didn't recognize, but whose voice seemed faintly familiar. "Not at your actions, but that you finally grew enough backbone to try to see them through…"

"Jefferson?" Morris's eyes darted back and forth with shock or fear. "How did you reinstate so quickly?"

"I have my secrets, as well…" He leaned over the control panel to the powerhouse. "You've solidified what truly must be done here today. May God have mercy on our souls… wherever they may be." With that, Jefferson pressed a series of red emergency stop buttons on the control panel.

Immediately the giant engines behind them began to shake the room as they ground to a halt.

"No!" Morris cried and leapt toward the control booth. He tried to force open the door. Finding it locked, he lashed at it with his club as the lights slowly began to flicker and fade.

Yellowcoats began stumbling and falling as the light grew dimmer.

Morris still seemed to have life in him, slamming at the door, trying to get in.

John gritted his teeth and charged the whitecoat, giving Morris a walloping right hook to the kidney. When he spun about in pain, John sent a fist to his jaw and decked Morris onto the floor of the powerhouse. He gurgled and wiggled, but then didn't seem to do much after that.

Suddenly the door to the control booth opened and a much younger version of Jefferson stepped out. He pressed something into John's hands. The book from earlier. He leaned heavily on John's shoulder. "You must leave quickly. The pumps have already stopped. The place will flood within minutes. You need to get to the elevator shaft and climb the maintenance ladder. Go past the ground floor landing. Go to the very top of the tower. You'll be safe there."

John nodded, not knowing what else to do.

"Please forgive us for what we have done." With that, his eyes went dim along with the lights in the powerhouse.

The hissing of residual pneumatics replaced the deafening engine roar. John found himself surrounded by the no-longer-living-but-not-quite-dead bodies of over a hundred yellow and whitecoats.

He grabbed a miner's hat and coat, secured the book inside his coveralls, and took off for the elevator shaft.

He found the tiny rung ladder next to the lift and began to climb with every bit of speed he could muster. He climbed in the darkness and utter silence, save for the dull glow of his headlamp and his breathing, which was now rasping and hoarse.

He climbed for what seemed like a mile, his arms feeling like they were weighted with lead. He felt something wet come from above. A splash of rain? More drops. He risked a glance up and noticed a thin trickle of water coming from above.

Had the water reached the mine already? He didn't know how much farther he had to climb before he reached the surface, but the mine would fill first. If he didn't get past the opening in time, he'd be flushed straight to the bottom.

The horrific thought of being buried alive by caustic seawater in the pits of this place reenergized his limbs. He climbed like a madman as the water falling from above began to increase. It started as a dribble and became a pour. The thunder of running water increased as the water grew into a waterfall, the acrid liquid making each rung slick like ice.

Suddenly something solid and heavy slammed into him from above. His foot slipped and he fell three rungs, slamming into them painfully before finally managing to grab hold and break his fall.

His ribs ached as he gazed up into the streaming caustic water and saw the writhing tentacles of a squid washed in by the stream. It lashed out with an arm which hooked onto the rung just above his head. He gritted his teeth, reached up, and grabbed onto the thing by the top of its mantle and pulled. It squealed in protest, its arms lashing back at him, their razor-sharp suction cups ripping at his coat.

He increased his strain, and all at once the mantle of the squid pulled free from its head. He let the body fall, its innards dropping past him and into the darkness below. The squid's head and tentacles convulsed for a moment and then finally lay still.

John continued his climb against the deluge, careful to skip the rungs containing the squid's remains. The torrent got worse as he climbed, his arms aching against the strain of the water. He pushed until at one point he had to hold his breath against the caustic deluge. His breath grew short. He felt as if he would pass out any moment. Panic set in, his instincts telling him let go and seek air.

He pushed forward. One more rung… one more.

His head burst through what felt like a layer of ice, and he breathed sweet air. He pushed on, realizing he was at the opening to the mine. A few rungs more and he cleared the water that was now streaming into the mine like a river.

He was exhausted, but dared not stay too close to the water's surface for fear of another squid reaching up and dragging him back down. He moved more slowly but didn't stop until he reached the very top of the elevator shaft. There he found the machine room, the massive electric motors which powered the lifts now dead.

From his vantage point of an open doorway, he could see as far as the seawall under the dull gloom of a murky night sky. Water filled the square well past the recess line as wave after wave crashed unabated over the wall. Tom and Jerry were still tethered to their posts and, remarkably, were still consuming their smaller cousins with no end in sight. He watched the incredible display and then slowly saw the tides turn.

As more and more water submerged them, the smaller squids gained the advantage, being more maneuverable than their larger immobilized cousins. The prey became predator and swarmed the giant cephalovores.

Tom broke free and, in a horrific display of fratricide, immediately attacked its still-tethered brother. It ripped and fed with a ferocity John had never seen before, an orgasmic display of cannibalistic gluttony. It was as if it were finally fulfilling its lifelong urge to taste the flesh of its sibling that it eyed and yearned for night after night. Even from his distance John could hear Jerry's fearful screeches as the giant cephalovore was devoured alive by its brother. Then came Tom's screams as they were both devoured by the sea of boiling squid.

The waves continued toward the mine, until it too was filled to capacity and the water level began to rise. John could think only of the feast the squid would have on the bodies below. He was thankful he had made it out alive.

Alive…

He could not appreciate that word until now.

Within an hour, the sea level had risen to two stories below where he lay. He felt suddenly isolated, like a man trapped in a cell surrounded by swarm of flesh-eating monsters. He slept but could get little rest with the constant wind and rain.

Hours passed.

He created a tent with his raincoat and used his headlamp's light to read passages from the book. Some of the pages were wet, but still readable. He read of God and of Christ Jesus, His Son, and he found himself praying to them as the hours turned into days.

Hunger and thirst brought on delirium and disorientation. He tried to read to pass the time, but he couldn't focus, and his lamp soon grew dim and died. He wondered if Morris had been right. Perhaps Jefferson was just a fool who had now destroyed the last refuge of mankind for this dream of pleasing God.

Eventually all he had strength for was sleep.

John awoke to a strange light. He opened his eyes and saw an eerie calm over the sea. He had no idea how much time had passed. He was frail, weakened. The light strained his vision, so bright. He managed to raise a hand to shield his face from it. He struggled to right himself on the wet concrete floor and slid toward the edge of the machine room, his prison cell above the sea monsters.

When he peered out, he was looking across an immense blue ocean. Light he had seen only in his dreams shone from the heavens in a massive white ball of warmth and beauty. Perhaps he was dead.

And then he saw something that convinced him that he had to be so.

A ship the size of a city was floating next to him. It was made of steel long rusted with age. He saw people, hundreds of them, running to and fro on the deck. The water level brought its bow right in line with the machine room, as if it had been designed that way.

John raised an arm to try and let them know he was there, but they were already busy maneuvering the great ship alongside the lonesome cell of his tower. After some minutes of yelling and whistling, he felt the floor shake as several sets of boots touched down within his cell.

He felt hands cradling him and easing him off the floor.

In his delirium he saw her amongst them. Dark chestnut skin and flowing ebony locks. The body of a dancer and the face of an angel. He reached out to her, and finally she saw him. Her face lit up as normal.

Jefferson had been wrong, after all. There was no miraculous divinity to his existence. No special gift of quickening from God to serve as a sign.

Here was his wife and his people who

lived beyond the sea. Wherever he'd come from, he had been found again. Even if he still couldn't remember them—all save the wife from his dreams.

He parted his cracked lips and strained with all his might to speak. His voice came out in a whisper, "*Ka...ren.*"

He expected her to smile, but her face paled and her eyes grew wide as if in fright. He panicked. Had he changed so much? Did she no longer recognize him?

She shared a fearful glance with the two men with her and then cautiously she looked back to John.

Finally she spoke, her voice soothing, lovely, smooth like satin.

"Who are you?" she said. "And how do you know my name?"


End


**Kirk Outerbridge** lives with his wife Ria and two sons Miles and Macen in beautiful Bermuda. He is a faithful member of the Church of Christ and is a professional engineer by training.

## A Model of Decorum
By Cindy Emmet Smith


Rose watched the golden afternoon wane. The pine trees at the edge of the garden stretched gnarled-finger shadows across the lawn. Soon the moon would rise. She unbuttoned her gown, removed it, then placed it folded on the end of her bed and stood in her shift. The clap of boots along the hall told her the warders were coming. She unfastened the silver cross that hung around her neck as they fumbled with the keys and opened the door.

"Good afternoon, Roberts."

"Good afternoon, miss."

Roberts wrapped her feet and ankles with strips of leather to protect them from the heavy manacles.

"Dunstan, I heard your wife was ill. How is she faring?"

"Much better, miss. I'll tell her you asked after her." Dunstan clamped another set of manacles around her wrists. "Are you ready?"

"As usual."

They each took an elbow and escorted her down the circular stairway to the cellars. She could feel the surge of change begin to throb in her veins—the warders must have felt it too, because they quickened their steps.

Here were the cells, and one—a cage of stone walls and iron bars—that was hers every month. A straw pallet graced one corner, and a shelf of rock set into the wall served as a table. It held the usual bucket of water, loaf of bread and iron cup. The warders led her in and fastened an iron girdle around her waist. A chain tethered her to a staple in the floor, but its coiled lengths allowed her to move freely and lie in the corner.

Dunstan held out the cup. "Drink up." Rose took it. "Don't forget the lantern." At least they let her have a light to keep the shadows lurking in the corners. Anything was better than the black time in this hole.

"No, miss." Roberts lit the iron lantern that hung from the center of the cellar with the candle he had carried with him. Dunstan fastened the bars to the cell, and they both left, closing the door behind them. No sound from her would disturb the residents upstairs.

She sat on the pallet, cradling the cup in her hands. The bitter taste of the drugs made her gag, but hopefully they would slow the change, maybe allow her to sleep . . . to dream of a time before the horror. . .

"Rose," her mother called, "How long does it take to pick a few vegetables?

Rose hurried to the door with a laden basket. Her mother grabbed it away and shoved another into her arms, followed by a small kettle with a lid.

"This is for Grandma Mya—she isn't well. See that you don't spill the soup. And don't dawdle in the woods with Michael or she'll never get her dinner."

"I won't dawdle, Mama, and I won't eat the cakes either." Rose kissed her mother's work-warmed cheek and hurried to the end of the path into the coolness of the woods.

She found Michael working near the crossroads. "I'm on my way to Mya's. Will you walk with me?"

Michael looked at the felled tree he was cutting, and at the shadows in the clearing. He scratched his head. "Not much more I can do today. I could walk with you."

# A Model of Decorum

"You can carry the basket." She thrust the basket into his hands and took hold of his elbow. Drawing in a deep breath, she let it out with a happy sigh and leaned against him as they walked.

A smile played across Michael's lips. "I'm thinking of asking your father if I may court you. Would he be agreeable to that, do you think?"

Rose felt her heart flutter. "Oh, he would be agreeable if he does not think sixteen is too young to wed."

"Then for now, I will court you so I will be ready when he thinks the wedding is timely."

Rose grabbed Michael's hand and tugged at him, but he reminded her of the soup she would spill, and she slowed to a sedate pace. They reached her grandmother's house while shadows still lay across the ground.

Rose rapped on the door.

"Grandmama, it's Rose. I've brought you supper. May I come in?"

Rose could barely hear Mya's weak assent. She pushed open the door. The room was dark and chilly, in spite of the warm day. She coaxed a little flame from the embers in the fireplace and lit a candle.

Mya huddled on the bed under a pile of quilts.

Michael checked the wood box. "I'll soon have some wood to fill this up. No wonder it's so cold in here."

"Thank you, young man. It's nice to get some help." Mya pushed herself up in the bed. "Come here, Rosie, and tell me about your beau."

"My beau, Grandmama?" Rose opened her eyes wide with surprise.

"I have eyes, don't I? I can see how he looks at you."

"His name is Michael—he cuts wood for the village. He's a craftsman too."

"Has he made your bridal bed yet?"

"Grandmama!"

"Don't sound so shocked, Rosie. I have ears, don't I? I could hear you whispering in the doorway."

"But Papa says . . ."

"I know what your Papa says, but things have to be done in their proper time —not after." She pulled Rose closer and gave her a kiss. "I know how you feel, my dear. I was a young girl too, believe it or not."

Rose wrapped her arms around Mya and returned the kiss. Michael came in with an armful of wood and the two soon had supper set out and a fire blazing.

Mya thanked them for the food. "Now you better get going; it's getting dark."

"But there's a full moon tonight," Rose protested.

"All the more reason we should be going," Michael added. "There are more than shadows in the woods at night."

"All right." Rose put the soup kettle in the basket and kissed her grandmother. Michael took her hand as they headed down the path.

The moon streamed light on the path, casting the shadows in crisp, black ribbons. They made their way easily to the crossroads, but Michael kept a lookout on either side of the path.

He kissed her on the forehead. "Hurry home now; I hear something in the dark."

"And you'll talk to my father tomorrow?"

"Naturally."

"Have a good night then. I'll go right home."

She had no sooner turned from Michael, than a shadow detached from the trees and blocked the path.

"What kept you, Rose?"

She yelped with surprise and peered into the dark. "Who is that? Peter?"

"It is. You and Michael were gone a long time. I've been waiting."

"What do you want?" She trembled in spite of the fact that she had known Peter all her life. She backed up, groping for Michael, but he had gone. Something in Peter's voice was harsh—off key.

"You." He stepped closer, hand outstretched.

"Why don't you come by our house tomorrow? It's late now—my mother will begin to worry."

"Do they worry about you? I thought you were a child of the forest, always wandering off the beaten path after a butterfly, or a flower." He grasped her elbow and fell into step beside her.

His hand felt hot, his grip bony, and Rose tried to shake him off. Since he didn't release her, she snatched his hand and pulled it off. But something was wrong— something in the skin and bones, something in the fur.

*Fur?* She gathered up her skirts and ran down the path. The basket slammed against her hip and she threw it aside. She didn't dare turn around—Peter could run faster and she didn't want to see him. She gasped for breath and tried to run faster. She didn't need to see him. She could hear him. His rasping breath soon scorched her neck. She felt his weight, his claws and rough fur as she fell to the ground.

"Michael—help!" Peter cut her cry short as he shoved her face into the ground. She tasted mud, then pain raked her shoulders and she sank into darkness.

As the darkness faded, she heard voices. They whispered and chattered like a flock of sea birds. Too fast—she couldn't understand them, only feel the urgency and grief. She turned her head, trying to shut them out, but they became louder, pounding into her skull with the throbs of pain. Tears filled her eyes and trickled down her face. "Mama," she sobbed.

"Sh, Rose, you don't have to talk. Drink a little water." She propped Rose's head and held a cup to her lips. "The doctor is coming."

"What happened?" She sipped, and then put her head down. Her back felt like fire.

"Don't you remember?" Her mother adjusted the pillows. "Michael carried you home and said he had killed a beast that attacked you in the woods. But when the men got there, they found Peter—dead."

The words—beast, Peter, dead—whirled through her mind. She wanted to scream with grief and confusion, but her throat closed and she let the world slip away.

Drumbeats woke her. Sunlight flowed through the window and pooled on the floor. It looked peaceful, but the voices outside sounded harsh and angry. And the drumbeats that punctuated the chaos heralded an execution.

"Rose, lie down, you're still hurt." Her mother tried to press her back into bed.

"What's happening? I hear drums."

"You don't want to see."

Wrapping a quilt around her, Rose hobbled to the window. "Michael? Why?"

"He killed Peter. You know our laws. One death requires another."

"He killed a beast, Mama. He was protecting me."

"There was no beast, dear, only Peter."

"I have to go."

"No, Rosie, don't watch."

# A Model of Decorum

"Get me a shift." She winced as her mother helped her lower the shift over her head and tie the neck. She pulled on a skirt, and picked up a thin scarf. A wave of dizziness overtook her, and she clutched the bedpost. "Mama, please help me. I have to see him."

She took hold of her mother's arm and they made a slow progress to the green where the scaffold stood ready. Around them, people whispered and moved aside. At the foot of the steps, Rose let go of her mother. She gripped the rail and mounted to the execution place. Michael's hands were tied behind his back, and the noose draped around his neck. His face was bruised and bloody, no doubt from the noisy crowds she had heard.

"Please go home, Rose. I don't want you to watch me die."

"I'm not going to watch you die." She turned and faced the crowd. "Michael did not kill a man!"

Shouts clamored around her. "There was no beast—only Peter."

"Listen to me. I swear it—there was a beast." She untied her shift and lowered it off her shoulders. Hot tears filled her eyes as she turned around. "No man could do

138

this."

No noise escaped the stunned crowd. The executioner stepped forward and replaced her shift. "But there was a death, and so there must be punishment."

"Banishment?" she whispered.

"So be it," he replied.

Rose faced Michael and lifted the noose off his neck. She smiled, and a split on her lip cracked open. Blood seeped into her mouth. She put her hand on the back of his neck, closed her eyes, and kissed him. "I love you, Michael." She tasted the salt of his blood as his bruised lips met hers.

"I love you, Rose." Blurred words escaped his damaged mouth.

"For always," she whispered.

"For always," he replied.

Mya stood by the fire as they entered the house. "Rose is coming home with me," she announced.

"Rose is hurt—she can't walk that far." Her mother protested.

"Rose's back is hurt, and her heart, not her feet. She's coming with me." Mya usually got her way.

"Mama, I want to go. It's peaceful there. I'll be fine."

# A Model of Decorum

Mya beckoned. "Come here child. I made some salve for you." She untied Rose's shift and eased it off her shoulders. She spread a fingerful of salve on her shoulders and smoothed it on. "Does that hurt?"

"No, it feels good."

"You are going to heal just fine." She padded the wounds with soft cotton and replaced Rose's shift.

"How did you know I was hurt?"

"I am an old woman—we are always the first to hear the whispers and stories." Mya put her lips next to Rose's ear and lowered her voice. "Come with me and I'll tell you everything."

Mya's house was quiet after the uproar in the village. Mya settled into her armchair and pointed to a stool by her feet. "Sit here, dear, and I'll comb your hair while I tell you what I know about the Wolf."

Rose sat down and pulled the pins out of her hair. Mya eased the snarls out with her fingers and picked up the comb. "Now I'm not talking about the grey wolves we see all the time, but a man—or woman— who takes on the form of a wolf when the moon is full. The Wolf must be nurtured by someone who knows the lore. Then they only live and hunt as the Wolf for the three days of the full moon. Peter may not have known he carried the seed, and when the rage came over him, he had no control. That is what you and Michael saw the other night, and that is what he killed. When this creature is dead, it changes back to the man."

"If he is dead, then the danger is past."

"Perhaps." The old woman stroked the comb through Rose's hair. "But this is the Wolf's forest, and there has been one here as long as the elders can remember. There may still be the one who seeded Peter, and Peter may have seeded you."

"Me?" Rose turned to look at her grandmother.

"The marks on your back are teeth and claw, and they are healing fast—faster than usual. It takes a few seasons for the full change to occur. Until then you will be safe here with me."

"Safe?" Rose shivered. "From what?"

"From a few who would be foolhardy enough to avenge Peter's death." Mya tied Rose's hair with a ribbon.

"What then? I don't want to end up like Peter."

"I have a recipe for a potion. It

prevents the change and helps to control the rage. If it doesn't help, I will take you to the hospital in Bridgeton."

"The asylum?"

Mya nodded. "Would it not be better to live as a mad person, than not at all?"

Rose put her head on Mya's lap. Her tears dampened her grandmother's apron, but Rose knew in her heart there was only one path.

There was a new warder. Rose followed him down the hall that itself had changed over the years, trying to recall his name, and how many different ones she had known over her time here. He held the door for her to enter the office.

"Name?" The man at the desk did not look up from his writing. Rose waited by the desk. Finally he lifted his head. "Name?" He repeated.

"I am Rose Aldren. And you?"

He set aside his pen and looked into her eyes. "I am Dr. Wellington, the new director of this facility. I'm sorry I did not introduce myself. Please take a seat."

Rose perched on the chair in front of the desk. "What do you want with me?"

"Treatments have changed in recent years. I am looking over every case to see what is needed and if there are new remedies that might be tried."

"I see."

"There are also a few patients who might benefit from a change of scene."

Rose waited. Dr. Wellington cleared his throat. "Are you a lunatic, Miss Aldren?"

"Indeed. My temperament is governed by the phases of the moon."

"That is not exactly what I meant." He made a note on the paper. "Do you consider yourself insane?"

"I can't answer that. I do not know the rule by which sane or insane is determined."

"Of course. That would be for the doctors to decide." He turned a page. "How long have you been a resident here?"

"I don't know. I stopped trying to keep track long ago. I do remember the day I came . . . I think I was eighteen years old. Dr. Johnston was the director then."

"That is not possible. You must have heard the warders speak of Dr. Johnston. He was the founder of this asylum. However, the records of your entry here have been lost. It is hard to believe you do not remember when it was, you hardly look older than twenty."

"Since I have no mirror, I can't tell how old I appear." Rose tried to suppress a smile, and kept her eyes averted. "I have heard that lycanthropy bestows long life and youthful appearance."

"Are you telling me you are a lycanthrope? In this modern day and age we do not give credit to legends and fairy tales."

"I beg your pardon. I simply stated a conception."

"Are you trying to provoke me, young lady?"

"No, sir." Rose raised her head to look at the doctor. "I am answering your questions."

"I see." He began shuffling through his papers, putting them in some order, neatly stacked together. Then he pushed aside the folder. "The attendants tell me you are a model of decorous behavior. Except, of course, for a couple of days a month. It is my belief that that can be controlled with proper medication."

Yes . . . bitter drugs in the water . . . something to induce sleep." Rose knew the taste of those powders.

"We have the formula for those drugs here. You should be able to obtain them yourself. In other words, Miss Aldren, we are sending you home."

"Home?" It had been so long since she had seen Mya's house in the forest, or their village with its homey farms and shops. When she closed her eyes, she could smell the wood fires and see the smoke that smudged the horizon.

"Yes," she replied. "I would like to go home."

Dr. Wellington shuffled a few papers.

"We do not have an address for any of your relatives. Where would you like to go?"

"My family is from River Run."

"River Run? Don't be silly. That town disappeared a hundred years ago."

Rose rubbed her forehead as tears filled her eyes. Was there nothing left?

"Is Helms Forest still standing?"

"Of course, it's a park now, but we need a more specific location."

"My grandmother had a cabin there— off Orchard Lane. The family would have maintained it. That is where I will go."

"I'll send for a car and driver." He

tapped a bell on the desk.

*Car?* How long had she been in this asylum?

"Dr. Wellington, if I may, I would prefer to walk. It isn't far, and the woods are pleasant this time of year."

Outside the red brick building of the asylum, one of her warders kindly led her through a fence made of metal wires in a crisscross pattern, unlike anything she had ever seen before. He pointed towards where he told her was south and gave her directions. Right, left, right. At unfamiliar street names.

Her walk took her past neatly arrayed houses in rows, carriages that moved without horses, and streets arranged in a grid pattern she did not recognize. How long had it been? Nothing was the same.

Her heart pounded in her chest as passersby in strange clothes stared at her. She found in herself the ability to smile at them with kindness, "Good day," she called out more than once. Only one answered, a scowling man with graying hair, with a brusque, "'morning."

When she arrived at the forest she found it had been hemmed in with more metal wire fencing in crisscross pattern. A sign stated the rules of behavior for visitors. They included no fires. No cutting wood. Her heart sank within her. The woods still existed, but so much had changed, so many things had been rebuilt. What were the chances the cabin still stood?

She walked through the forest. The path had changed, some trees alongside it were taller and there were fewer trees overall. Still, she recognized the path. She followed it in the direction where the cabin once had been.

She came to another stretch of wire fence, reaching the end of the forest park without seeing the cabin, her heart in dismay. Yet the path continued outside the fence. And unlike on other sides of this protected forest, which was surrounded by streets which contained only a relatively few carefully planted trees, a small patch of wild wood stood here, outside the park. Passing through the fence, her eyes caught sight of a cabin. *The* cabin.

As she neared it, she heard the chunk of axe on wood and her heart quickened. She smelled a whiff of smoke on the breeze and when she rounded the corner, there was Michael, his arms loaded with

# A Model of Decorum

logs. Her blood must have transferred to him in that kiss.

He saw her and his old grin spread across his face. Together they could hold the forest for the wolf.

End

**Cindy Emmet Smith** is a prize-winning writer from central Pennsylvania where she lives with her kilt-wearing husband. Their three children have flown the nest.

She published the novel *The Cracked and Silent Mirror in 2000*. Services appeared in "Church Worship magazine" in 2002 and 2003, stories in "True Confessions" and Coming Home from Rocking Chair Reader in 2004 and poetry in "Time of Singing," "Byline," and "Penned from the Heart." She contributes to the Christmas section of the Williamsport Gazette which was edited by West Branch Christian Writers. Cindy currently has two speculative fiction novels available: *Perfect Blood Innocent Blood* and *Solo Flight*.

**Dental Troll**
By Lisa Godfrees

The only thing good about losing a tooth—Alexa's tongue probed the tender coppery tasting vacancy in her mouth—was a visit from the tooth fairy.

Or so her parents claimed.

They'd insisted that if she wiggled her tooth every day, the boney stalactite would come out on its own, and the tooth fairy would visit to swap treasures.

Wiggling it hurt, so she'd ignored the dangling, wobbly nuisance until her father finally had enough. Out came the dental floss, followed by a miniature torture session. The spectacle ended with a bloody tooth in her hand and an aching hole in her mouth.

Alexa placed her molar inside the tulle bag and cinched the closing strings. Her tongue found her other loose molar—the one her parents didn't know about. She had to find a less painful way to get rid of it. Tonight was her chance.

Alexa awoke to shaking and muffled

grunting coming from her pillow. She shot up and snapped on her bedside lamp. The pillow stilled.

Her trap must have worked! She raised her pillow and froze.

A tiny creature struggled against the straps of her double drawstring bag. He was the size of her palm, but brown and ruddy like the knot of an old oak tree. Dressed in murky overalls and a mildewed cap, he could have been the love child of a toad and leprechaun.

Alexa cleared the sleep from her throat. "Are you the tooth fairy?"

"Do I look like a fairy to you?" His raspy voice was surprisingly deep for such a small being. "And don't you know it's bad luck to catch a dental troll?"

"I've never heard of a dental troll."

He snorted. "Figures. That tooth fairy propaganda has worked too well."

"The tooth fairy's not real?"

"Of course not. She's a marketing ploy to get people to leave their teeth for us." He struggled against her little bag. "Ever since the Dental Accords of 632, we've been prohibited from dental mining on pain of death. Now let me out of here."

"What do you do with the teeth?"

"We eat them, of course. What do you think dental trolls live on?"

"How would I know? I've never heard of you before, remember?"

Fairies were supposed to be good, but what about dental trolls? Could she trust him with her request? Her tongue prodded her loose tooth again and she winced.

"Promise me a favor, and I'll let you go."

The little troll scowled, making his already ugly face repugnant. "What?"

She paused, carefully wording her request. All the fairy tales she read claimed phrasing was important. "You can have my baby teeth if you can remove them without hurting me. Do you have a spell for that or something?"

"No spells. I'm not a fairy, remember?" he mocked. "But I can take your teeth like we did in the old days. You won't feel a thing."

"Really?"

"I promise." He beamed, revealing two rows of crooked stone teeth. "So is it a deal?"

Apprehension settled in her stomach like lead, but what choice did she have?

"Okay."

# Dental Troll

Alexa retrieved her small pair of craft scissors and cut the troll loose from the bag.

"Now it's your turn." He gestured to her pillow.

"You swear it won't hurt?"

"You'll be asleep the whole time."

She lay down on her bed as directed. He spoke a thick, heavy word. One that sounded like distant thunder in a cave deep underground. The last thing she saw as her eyelids drooped was his sneering face leaning over her, a small pickaxe in his hand.

Sunlight broke through her curtains and pulled Alexa awake. She ran her tongue over her gums and gasped. Something seemed wrong. She scrambled to the mirror.

All of her teeth were gone—baby and permanent! Bloody craters remained where her beautiful teeth had been.

The little troll had lied to her! He was only supposed to take her baby teeth. Wasn't that the deal?

She sobbed, bloody drool escaping from her mouth and tears streaming down her face. Only one thing worked out as promised: she hadn't felt a thing.

End

**Lisa Godfrees** is fascinated with creatures that don't exist, especially Jackalopes. She was a forensic scientist for over a decade and still testifies as a technical expert in the courtroom. She is a light programmer extraordinaire, incredibly punny, an oxford comma enthusiast, mom of two, wife of one, hybrid homeschool parent and self-proclaimed data junkie. She's also the author of about a half dozen great short stories featured in anthologies as well as the co-author of *Mind Writer*. Connect with her at LisaGodfrees.com.

## HMS Mangled Treasure
*Or **The Rescue of Mr. Spaghetti***
By L. Jagi Lamplighter Wright

"Pirates, you say?" asked the detective who stood on Clara's front stoop. At least Clara thought he was a detective, since he wore a fedora and a trench coat and looked disturbingly like a Humphrey Bogart clone. He could have been the claims adjuster, however. She had talked to so many people, she had lost track.

Clara put her fists on her hips. "Listen here, Buster. Maybe you want me to lie to you – like that punk of an ex of mine did last time this happened. Tell you some comfortable story about car thieves and let it go at that. But that ain't gonna happen!" She shook her head for emphasis, sending her many cornrows flying and wagged a finger at him. "I'm one woman who respects the truth, and that. Is. Not. Going. To. Change!"

Usually, this was the place where they shot her the "you should be locked away" look. This guy just nodded calmly, like he was on the set of Dragnet or something. Cool as a cucumber, he was.

"Pirates towed your car, Ma'am. Is that

right?" he asked again. He spoke with a Bronx drawl, so that his "that" sounded like "dat". Clara had never heard a Bronx accent in real life. She kept expecting him to drop it and talk like a real human being.

"Yes!" she snapped.

"That's all right, Ma'am. I believe you."

"You...you do."

"Sure thing, Ma'am. These pirates have been towing cars all over town."

Clara sighed. It felt good to have someone believe her for a change. It had been a while since anyone had believed her about anything. Still, it took all the fight out of her.

"Any idea who's behind it?" she asked as nicely as she was able.

The detective nodded solemnly. "A pack of the worst supernatural scum in Fairydom."

Just great. It would be that the guy who finally believed her was three crayons short of a box. Clara cocked her head and fixed him with the look that her miserable excuse of an ex used to call the Hairy Eye.

"Faeries towed my car?"

The detective met her gaze square on, completely unfazed by the Hairy Eye. That in itself was amazing.

"Ma'am," he drawled. "you just told me that Pirates stole your car and sailed away – in the middle of Chicago, and I believed you. Common etiquette dictates you should extend to me the same courtesy."

Clara frowned. The guy seemed calm and reasonable. Not what she expected from a crazy, but then she had been an ER doc, not a psychiatrist. Maybe real crazies were as cool as cucumbers. It would certainly explain why he dressed and talked as if he had walked out of a 1940s movie.

"Look here, Mr. Spade-wanna-be. Pirates is one thing…" Clara froze, her mouth wide open, because at that moment, she remembered something.

A terrible sensation spread through her body, much like what she imagined it might feel like to be stung by scorpions. Tears pricked threateningly at her eyes. She let out a low warble of a moan.

"Mr. Spaghetti!" she wailed. "He's locked in the car!"

"Is that your dog, Ma'am?" the detective asked.

Clara shook her head, nearly whipping him with her cornrows. Next time, she would stand a little closer and wap him good.

"No. A doll. My son's favorite doll." It shamed her that her voice broke. "He's going to be inconsolable."

"Children lose dolls all the time, Ma'am. Part of life."

Clara turned on the poor man, showing her teeth like a wolf. "Is that so? Why don't you come home and explain it to my son. He's eight years old, weighs nearly seventy pounds, and has the language capacity of a delayed two-year-old. You come over to my house tonight, and you explain to Sammy what happened to his Mr. Spaghetti!"

The detective lowered the brim of his fedora. "I'll get your car back, Ma'am."

Clara lay on her stomach among the trees at the Lincoln Park Zoo and peered through her binoculars. The ground was damp and cold under her shirt. She hoped this would not take too long.

According to her research into recent car thefts – she had called her sister's hunky friend at the police department – the roadside parking area she had under surveillance was a likely spot for the car thieves to hit and just after morning rush hour was a likely time. Pre-dawn would have been better, but she had been forced to wait until after her own two kids, Sari and Sammy, had left for school.

Twelve cars had disappeared from this parking area alone in the last week. Like hers, they had all been parked off by themselves, with no one behind them. Of course, that did not mean one would disappear today, while she was watching, but she could hope.

And hope she did! It had taken a whole boatload of effort to rearrange her schedule so she could have today off. It would be weeks before she could arrange another free day. She had to horde her precious time off for when Sammy was home. It was hard enough to arrange things so that she did not have to work weekends.

To judge from last night's reaction, her household would not survive another day without Mr. Spaghetti, much less weeks! Clara rubbed the bump on the bridge of her nose from where it had broken during the fit Sammy threw the last time Mr. Spaghetti went missing two years ago, the time they had accidentally left the rag-doll at the grocery store. She used to have a beautiful nose. People on the street would stop her and tell her how she could be a model. Of course, that was ten years and forty pounds ago. Today, she had more important things to worry about than whether her looks could make strangers gawk.

Besides, what had her looks ever gotten her except her good-for-nothing ex?

Clara lowered her head, resting it on her hands. How had her life come to this? Ten years ago, it had been filled with such promise!

She had grown up in the slums; no one in her family had ever finished high school. No one in her family had ever amounted to much of anything, until Clara came along.

Clara had finished high school. She had finished college. She had gone all the way through seven years of medical school. Clara had become a doctor! When her Mamma was young, women did not become doctors, much less women of color. Yet, Mamma's little girl had become one of the top physicians in the Mercy Hospital Emergency Room. She had saved lives!

She still had a vase of dried flowers on her mantelpiece, the remnants of the first bouquet given to her by someone whose life she saved.

She had given all this up for Sammy.

Clara recalled back to when Sammy was a baby. He had been the sweetest thing in the early months, even happier and less troublesome than his older sister, Sari. Even the Second Coming of Christ Himself could not have been sweeter.

But by two, he still was not talking, and he had started doing things with his hands, odd things that made him stand out from other children, holding them funny and waving them in front of his face. By five, he still was not talking, he still did weird things with his hands, and he was still throwing fits – the kind of fits her friends' children had stopped throwing at three or four. Then, her so-called-friends stopped bringing their children over to play with Sammy.

And the screaming! Bright lights set him off. Cleaning products in the air set him off. Dyes in the food set him off. And not being allowed to eat the brightly colored candies the other children ate?

That set him off the worst of all.

At first, Stan went into denial. He tried to cover for Sammy, when the boy was young, to hide it. But by the time he had a six-year old, who was still in diapers and who bent over and gestured oddly while moaning in public, even Stan, Master of De Nile himself, could not hide it anymore. He started saying that Sammy was not his son, even accused Clara of having an affair!

Her, Clara, the ultimate good girl! Boy, she let him have it for that one!

Of course, it had not always been like that. Once, Stan had been the husband she was so proud of, so handsome and buff. She gave the tear on her cheek a vicious wipe. Did no good to focus on the past. Just made a girl feel sad. Had to stay focused on the present.

It had been her decision to leave the ER and stay home full time to take care of Sammy that had really ruined things. Stan did not like losing the status of his doctor wife, and he did not like losing her six digit paycheck, not one bit. He tried to have Sammy put in an institution. When Clara would not go along, he bugged out. Took his sorry ass and ran.

Well, good riddance to him! She didn't need a man like that anyhow.

Stan sent money, but it was never enough. He spent most of what he made on his new wife and their perfect little girl. Clara was reduced to working at Smarty-Mart.

Smarty-Mart! From a top Emergency Room physician to the manager at a Smarty-Mart. It was enough to make a lesser woman cry.

But Clara was not a lesser woman. She was a survivor. If sacrificing her hard-won career to become a manager at the Smarty-Mart was what God required in order to give her son a good life, that was what she was going to do!

It did not mean that she did not break down and bawl like a baby now and then —usually at night when no one was awake to see. But she sure as heck did not sit around grousing about what life had thrown her way, like some people she knew.

By and large, now that she thought about it, that was true of all the mothers of "Special Needs" children she knew. Being active upon her son's behalf had led her to meet a lot of other mothers of children with problems "in the spectrum." They were a surprisingly resilient lot – not counting the one or two who could not hack it. There was a reason that their mutual support group was called Mothers From Hell.

It was all worth it of course. Sammy might not be like other children. He might not talk clearly. He might flail his limbs when he got upset, sometimes even hurting his mother or sister. All that vanished, however, when she looked at him and saw his steady, shining eyes gazing back at her with such love, such trust.

It was like gazing directly at his soul, like looking into the eyes of an angel. One smile from Sammy made all the crap worth it!

From somewhere above the tree tops came a very strange sound. Clara stiffened and listened. Voices, she thought, like a chorus. Only the voices were cold and eerie and soulless and filled with a harsh glee that had nothing to do with gladness.

*The crew of the Mangled Treasure are we*
*Fearless and peerless and wicked and free!*
*Deathless and pitiless robbers are we*
*Our hearts be as restless and cold as the sea!*

# HMS Mangled Treasure

*We do not bleed blood and we cannot weep tears!*
*Our hearts are as empty and deep as our years!*

"This one will do, Lads!" called out a single deep gravelly voice.

Clara brought the binoculars up to her eyes and stared. Her jaw gaped. Even though she had caught a glimpse of these thieves before, it had not prepared her for what she saw now.

A huge, square-rigger with sails the color of swamp fog mist sailed down out of the cloudy sky. The mainmast bore the symbol of a bleeding moon and a Jolly Roger flew from the foremast. Aboard the vessel was a crew of pirates, but not like the pirates in any book or movie.

Short, squat men in long jackets and boots with crimson sailors' hats, served as powder monkeys. They toiled to and fro carrying rocks to the cannons. Huge, hulking creatures manned the guns, their tri-cornered hats, vests, and breeches were of bark and dead leaves. Tiny, winged pixies, no bigger than Clara's finger, swarmed about the lookout. They were not cute, pretty creatures, like from a story book, but cruel, nasty, little things with ugly, distorted faces. In their hands, they held shiny copper cutlasses.

At the helm stood a leering old man with a long white beard. He was covered in barnacles and seaweed and wore a conch shell for a hat. To his left, a horrifyingly ugly creature with an enormous nose and no mouth at all. It leaned precariously over the railing, holding what appeared to be a pistol made of wood.

The captain and his officers were of another cut. Clara trained her binoculars upon them in fascination. These tall haughty faeries, as handsome as sin, were decked out in pirates' garb of capes, jackets, blousy shirts, bright sashes, and high boots. Only the capes were tattered and flowing, the blousy shirts were diaphanous, and the wide sleeves of their jackets hung down like the specter's shroud. The whole ensemble looked not so much like pirates as masqueraders at an eerie Venetian ball impersonating pirates.

On the side of the hull, scripted in flowery loops, was *The Mangled Treasure*. Red Caps threw down copper hooks, green with patina, that caught on a tree and a bicycle rack.

"Heave! Heave!" the crew shouted

harshly. Three large burly trolls winched the ship down to the ground. The tree swayed wildly. Atop, Red Caps and pixies reefed the mainsail and the foresail. With a rusty creak, the stern of the ship opened outward, descending until it touched the ground where it formed a ramp.

The harsh crack of a whip made Clara jump. A huge creature, muscle-bound and awkward, stumbled forward; one big red eye peered out from the middle of its head. It was bound in chains. A huge, spiked, bronze collar surrounded its neck and similar rings encircled each wrist and each ankle. The greenish chains were held by many Red Caps, each anchored by a troll.

That was a cyclops, from Greek mythology! What was it doing on a ship run by nightmares out of the Brothers Grimm?

The horrible creature with the ghoulish, mouthless face held the whip. It drove the cyclops down the ramp. Shuffling slowly, the one-eyed brute moved to the red Chevy parked by itself and secured the vehicle with the hooks. Then, it shuffled up the ramp again, grunting under the onslaught of lashes when it paused, and began turning a crank. Slowly, with jerks and stops, it winched the car up onto the deck.

Then, the captain gave the signal. An unseen mechanism hoisted up the stern ramp and the faerie square-rigger floated eerily upward. Atop, the pixies raised the sails, and the ship shot off over the buildings, straight up into the cloudy sky, which was darkening into night.

Clara lowered her binoculars and stared after the departing faerie ship, her body trembling. That detective guy had been right. She owed him an apology.

She stared after the ship for a long time, fear warring with determination. Then she stood up, shook herself, and headed across town to wait for the library to open.

By the time Clara scrunched down on the floor of her rental car and spread the blanket over her head, it was already dark. She rested her head against her old gym bag – from the days when she had time for things like going to the gym. The bag was stuffed with the goodies she had bought after her trip to the library, things the books at the library had suggested she might need.

As she waited in the dark, under the blanket, in the chilly, smelly car, she prayed. Her great faith in the existence of God had never wavered, not through all the curve-balls life had thrown her. She just no longer trusted that God would answer her prayers. Still, it did no harm to ask. He was a God of Mercy, maybe he would take pity on her plight.

More likely, of course, he was laughing his Divine rear off.

The car lurched and bumped. Clara's stomach tensed. Was it them?

She grabbed her gym bag tight with one hand and braced herself against the seat with the other. There was a moment of stillness accompanied by a low clanking sound. Then the car began to move. As it swayed in the air, Clara snorted with sad amusement: first prayer answered in eight years, and God picks her request to be kidnapped by faerie pirates.

Clara lay very still, listening for the sound of retreating feet. The ride on the faerie square-rigger took about half an hour according to her cell phone. Then the car had been lowered again into its current location. There had been some banging around, some muffled voices, and a loud scraping sound. Then, everything went quiet.

Very slowly, Clara pushed the blanket aside and sat up. She crawled onto the back seat and peered through the window. Another car sat next to hers, and then another and another and another. She sat up higher and peered farther. No one seemed to be about. Opening the door, she climbed out and shimmied up on to the roof of the rental, shading her eyes to help her see in the pale moonlight.

There were cars as far as she could see. The sea of cars spread out from her current position in all directions except to the left, where a tall building stood. In the other direction, toward the edge of her vision, she saw a couple of boats standing among the vehicles. To the right of that, near what might be a road, was that…a plane?

How would she ever find Mr.

Spaghetti?

Jumping down, Clara gave the rental car a fond goodbye pat. With the loss of this car went her very last credit card, the one she had been keeping for emergencies, in case one of the kids got really sick and needed more doctoring than their mother could provide.

She shrugged and threw the strap of the gym bag over her shoulder. She crept quietly forward, peering into each car as she went, shivering a little despite her inside-out sweatshirt – that was one of the tricks she had picked up during her time in the library. Wearing your clothes inside out was supposed to keep Faeries at bay. From time to time, she stopped and listened, but she could hear nothing except the hum of a freeway in the distance. She soon realized that her current efforts were futile. The gibbous moon was not bright enough to let her distinguish the details of individual cars at a distance. There was no way to spot her car from afar and far, far too many cars to search individually.

Setting off for the huge building she had glimpsed to the left, Clara swore solemnly that if she ever got her car back, she would buy one of those little Disney figures at Smarty-Mart that snapped onto the antenna to help you find your car in a crowded parking lot. A new electronic opener—something she could point and click, and her car would light up—would be even better, but those cost a pretty penny. More pennies than were in her piggy bank.

The bay door led into some kind of warehouse or factory. She could not see much, stumbling around in the dark, but it must have been a large place, because every object she accidentally knocked or kicked echoed eerily. She needed to find a light switch. She flicked her gym bag in annoyance and snorted. All this clever gear, and she had not thought to bring a flashlight. And her piece-of-crap pay-as-you-go cellphone didn't have a large enough screen to illuminate anything but her foot.

After bashing her head on some hanging thingamajig, Clara finally found a door leading to another room. On the far side of the door, she found a light switch, only now she no longer needed it.

Before her stretched a foundry. It was

dimly lit, but the bright orangey glow of molten metal illuminated the vast area, making it look like a nightmare about the fourth circle of Hell. The place smelled of hot metal and was warm, a welcome change from the chill of the night. Clara moved forward cautiously, glad she had paused before flicking the switch. She was obscured by shadows that would have vanished had she blunderingly flicked on a new light source.

From her position, she could not see the work force. However, work force there must have been, because huge cranes were lowering cars – full size sedans and SUVs – into the molten vats. Far above the factory floor, a wooden command center hung out over work area, supported by buttresses. Clara stopped beneath it and gave the structure the Hairy Eye. Who would be kooky enough to use burnable materials, instead of steel or glass, in an environment so filled with fiery sparks? Faeries, of course, who cannot touch cold iron – and apparently not hot iron either.

If the faerie overlords were not willing to come onto the factory floor, of what did the work force consist? More enslaved cyclopes?

With a loud grinding creak, one of the vats tipped. A stream of hot yellow liquid poured into some kind of long trough, illuminating more of the building. Shadows fled from the corner around her. Clara saw something pale dangling on the wall to her right. She moved to investigate. "Dear God!" She pressed her hand against her mouth, hard.

Hanging suspended by a rope was the detective who had questioned her the previous day, the one who had promised to get her car back. He hung by his wrists, dangling above a circle of toadstools that grew directly from the cement. His face had been beaten. He had a black eye and an ugly bruise on one cheek. He did not seem to be breathing. "Is he…are you dead?"

"Nah, it's okay, Ma'am." The voice came from some place to the left of the body. It sounded as if a pair of cymbals had been granted a voice and were speaking with a Bronx accent. "That's just my body. Normally, I stay in there. I kinda got out of it, on account as I did not like the way they was treating it."

"What…what are you?" Clara's hand was already in the gym bag, reaching around for some kind of weapon. She pulled some things out at random and found herself holding a bell and a carton of salt. Would that work? The fairytales had not been very specific on the subject of what worked on who.

"Ever read The Tempest, by that Spearshaker guy?" His voice now issued from the air above the closest point of the toadstool circle. When Clara nodded, he continued. "Remember Ariel? Well, I'm his...you'd call it a brother. Only I spend my time in this body here, on account of Mr. Prospero wanting me to be able to help you humans. He's the one who decided I was to be a detective. Name is Mab, by the way."

"Mab?" Clara looked to and fro, but could see no sign of the speaker, which made sense, she supposed, if he was some kind of spirit of air. She crossed her arms. "I thought that was the Faerie Queen's name?"

"Nah, her name was Maeve. Spencer got a little confused."

"I see. Can I get you down?" Clara took a step forward, eyeing the toadstools dubiously. "I brought some herbicide."

"Herbicide? Clever! A girl after my

own heart. You'll probably need it, but don't use it here. There are other spells, you might get hurt."

"What can I do?"

The voice was silent for a moment. Then, with a sigh, he said. "Ma'am, I'm going to ask you a favor. I realize you might not be able to grant it, but I…I gotta ask."

"Go ahead," Clara eyed the air suspiciously. "Worst I can do is say no."

"In order to get anything out of here, you're going to have to face the faeries. Faeries don't got free will – well not in the way that a creature with a soul does. They are constrained to obey certain rules."

"Like them leaving a poor soul alone if his clothes are inside out, or not crossing a circle of salt?" Clara asked. What had seemed warm when she first stepped in from outside was now growing uncomfortably hot. She wiped sweat from her brow.

"Right! And they have to stick to the rules under which they operate, whether they like it or not. And they're tricky. Comes from having no hope of Heaven, you know; no reason to behave. If you survive whatever they throw at you, they'll let you pick one thing to take away with you. Pick me."

Clara drew her head back and stared at him like he was bonkers. "Pick you, not my car with Mr. Spaghetti?"

"Pick me, Ma'am, cause once I get out of here, I can shut this place down. Shut it down forever. Put...let's just say I can put everything back where it goes – I could do it now, if I could get to my danged cell phone, but I can't work it in this form, and you can't cross the magic circle to get it for me.

Mab's voice became more serious. "If you pick something else, Ma'am you'll get to leave with it, but everything else will stay here. Until...some other mortal happens upon me, I guess. I could be here a very long time. Not that that's your problem."

"What's the number? I could call them." Clara offered, pulling out her phone.

The voice sounded truly embarrassed.

"No one commits numbers to memory any more."

Clara put her hands on her hips and snorted. "You think that's going to be hard, Detective Mab. On one hand, I get a doll or a car. On the other hand, I get both the doll, my car, the rental, and I save you, another human be…another living being. And you think I'm going to find this decision hard?" She waggled her head at him. "You have another thing coming."

The detective's voice was low and sad. "Ma'am, you have no idea. If you chose to ask for me, I swear I will do everything in my power to return…everything here that is yours. But if you do not, I'll understand. Mortals can only bear so much."

Clara held up her hand, as if she were saying the Pledge of Allegiance. "I give you my solemn word I will ask for you. There. How's that! I am a woman of integrity. I. Do. Not. Break. My. Word."

"You shouldn't have done that, Ma'am…but thank you."

She slipped around the wall and was about to head up the stairs to the command room when she saw it. Her car! It sitting in the line of cars waiting to be turned into slag. Clara flew down the stairs that led to the waiting area. She hunkered down and ran between the vehicles like a spy in the movies. Reaching hers, she fumbled with her keys, breathing hard. Then, she had the door open.

A lunge into the back, and Mr. Spaghetti was in her hands!

Clara shut the door and sat down, leaning against the tires of the next car over, a huge green van. She hugged the stupid, tattered rag-doll to her chest, its fingerprint-stained, spaghetti-like hair flopped against her shoulder.

"You caused me a whole whopper of trouble, Buddy O!" she whispered to the silly thing. "I don't know what my son sees in you, but he loves you."

But that was the way of love, was it not?

Clara gave the rag doll a last fierce hug and shoved it in her bag. She wiped the sweat from her face again. What to do now? If it were not for the detective, she would just leave now. Forget the car, forget that she had ever seen anything like this. Just get the doll back to Sammy and life could go back to normal...without a car or a credit card. But she felt bad just abandoning the guy. Maybe she should try the herbicide on the toadstools after all.

Wiping a stray tear from her eye that had crept out when she was hugging the doll, she rose to her feet. As she did so, she glanced toward the factory floor.

Where had all the children come from?

Clara's feet did not move toward the door. Instead, they crept closer to the factory floor.

It was like walking into a Dickensian nightmare. Children, from tiny three year olds to burley teens, worked the factory, moving levers, throwing switches, changing the molds into which the molten metal poured. Dirty children, dressed in rags, with bruises and open sores. Sweaty children, working in all that heat. Dull-eyed children, who went through their routines without any sign of that spark that made a child well…a child.

Human children. Enslaved by faeries. Here in the modern day, in the country of freedom! Children. Little children, like Sammy. Like Sari. One of the little dark boys even reminded her of Sammy.

Despite the heat, an icy, cold chill traveled own her spine.

No, not reminded her – this boy looked like Sammy. Exactly like Sammy. Except, he looked like what Sammy would look if he were an ordinary child– without that sometimes stupid, sometimes beneficent expression the real Sammy usually wore. Like what Sammy looked like when he concentrated hard, and you could not tell that there was anything amiss with him. Like what Sammy would look like with a festering wound on his cheek and forehead.

That boy out there, with burn marks on his wrist where molten sparks had caught him—the bastards did not even give the children leather gloves—looked exactly like her son.

How could that be?

Clara examined the rest of the children she could see. Her heart nearly stopped. There! That little girl was a spitting image of Jillian, the sole little girl in the ABA program at Sammy's school. And behind the giant crane! The boy who was missing an arm. He looked like the twin brother of Nicholas, from that Special Need's exercise class she used to drag Sammy to.

Slowly, her legs gave way. Clara sank to the cold cement floor and bowed her head. In all her years of medical school and ER work, Clara had never chucked her cookies. She had been proud of that. Her Stomach of Iron failed her now. She vomited behind the tire of a white BMW.

Crouching down, she grabbed her knees and stayed there until her legs stopped shaking. Then, slowly she stood up and made herself look again.

She knew how this could be. She had only just read all those faeries stories.

Hot tears splashed from her cheeks to the floor. Her life, her wonderful career, the lives she might have saved, the husband she had – yes, she would admit it now, she had loved Stan before it all went wrong, and the coward ran out on her – all thrown away so she could raise a faerie impostor, who had been left in place of her real son.

Her Sammy was a changeling.

Now that she knew, her life finally made sense. Laughing in the face of discipline. Weird behaviors. Lack of empathy with human beings. Was that so different from laughing at funerals and the other bizarre things faeries were wont to do in tales?

And modern chemicals? Bright lights? Of course, her son could not tolerate them! He was a freaking faerie! In retrospect, she wondered why she had not figured it out sooner.

Were they all changelings? Over a

million autistic children in America alone. Had they all been stolen by faeries?

She thought of her friend Jenna, patiently enduring the screaming and fits of her three autistic boys. She thought of Martha, who spent her days driving from one doctor to another, determined to find the illusive missing cure. She thought of Mrs. O'Conner, whose daughter had bugged out, leaving her to raise her two autistic grandchildren.

All these women, all that labor and love, wasted on changelings – while their own children suffered as slaves.

"Samuel!" she took off at a run, sprinting across the factory floor. "Samuel!"

The little boy turned as she approached. His eyes grew large. Staring up at her in wonder, he asked in a small voice. "Are you…my mama?"

Clara grabbed him and clasped him to her heart. "I am! I am your Mama! And I'm never going to leave you again!"

She knelt and hugged him, her missing son, her long lost beloved child. He smelt like metal fumes and smoke, but under that was a scent that reminded her of hugging Sari. This little boy smelt like her daughter!

Any doubts Clara might have had evaporated. The two of them hugged and cried and cried.

A scrabbling noise startled Clara, just as a Red Cap lunged for her. Screaming, Clara threw her body between the Red Cap and her son. Frantically, she stuck her hand into the gym bag, feeling around for something of use. The Red Cap let out a squeal of frustration. His hands clawed at her but did not touch her.

Her clothes! The inside-out clothes! They had worked. Losing no time, Clara grabbed her son, pulled off his soiled shirt, and turned it inside out. Putting it on him again, she too off, sprinting toward the cars and the stairs and door out beyond.

More Red Caps appeared. One wore a cutlass. One swung a copper rope. Another held two wooden belaying pins like daggers. Soon three chased her, then four. As she neared the automobiles, she saw a fifth Red Cap standing straight ahead of her, grinning. Clara ground to a stop, hugging her boy tight. She had deliberately looked up Red Caps in the library. What had that big black book claimed countered them? She rooted around in her bag for her cheat sheet.

Oh, right! Bible verses. Made them stop and loose a tooth or some such. Clara blurted out the only Bible passage she could bring to mind.

"Give us this day our daily bread!"

The five advancing Red Caps stopped cold. Moaning, they grabbed their jaws and writhed. A moment later, a tooth popped from each of their mouths. The teeth shot across the room, bouncing off of the floor and ricocheting off of vats. From the additional moans and pings she heard beyond the range of her sight, she assumed more Red Caps had been on the way.

During all this, Clara had not been idle. She grabbed the Morton carton and spun in a circle, letting the salt pour out liberally. Then, she spun around again, to make sure she had not missed a spot. She had to pour salt on the two gaps she found, but, finally, she had a closed circle.

The Red Caps rushed up and crowded around her safe space. They were short, bearded men in dark sailor's suits, wearing red sailor's caps and each missing a tooth.

They shuffled around the circumference, as if searching for a weakness.

"Hey, little men?" Clara called. When

they gathered around to hear her, she shouted, "Boo!" and gave them the Hairy Eye, the real deal, with the full force of her scorn.

The Red Caps scattered like leaves before a leaf blower.

"Now that's how it's supposed to work!" Clara hooted triumphantly, her confidence returned. "God only knows what was up with that detective. He didn't even blink!"

From the far side of the factory came a curtain of sparkling lights. This glittering pixy dust sprinkled like rain onto any children that got in its way. These children slowed and stood still. Some stared blankly, others slumping and falling to the ground, asleep. Clara grabbed her frightened son close and murmured, "Salt, don't fail me now!"

As the curtain of sleepy sand approached, Clara saw that a platoon of pixies flew above, dropping the pixy dust from little pouches they carried on their belts. The pixies flew directly toward her. There was nowhere to run. Clara gritted her teeth and stood tall.

The glittering wall of golden dust struck the circle of salt and curved, until

Clara and Samuel seemed to be surrounded by a semi-circular curtain of shimmering light. But neither the pixies nor the dust crossed the salt.

"Hot dang!" Clara grinned widely. "Those library books rock!"

The pixy dust hung in the air a time, like motes in a beam of light, then it slowly sank to the ground, forming a sparkly, golden semi-circle around her white circle. Samuel looked up from where Clara had pushed him against her body, his eyes wide. "What happens now, Mama?"

"Don't know, Pumpkin. We wait."

"I'm scared, Mama."

"I'm here with you, Baby." She smoothed his curly hair. "I'm not gonna leave you!"

A door opened in the wooden command center, and the captain emerged. He began floating down. Clara scowled. The ship's name had seemed kind of amusing when she read it in the park. It did not seem at all amusing now.

The captain was tall and fae, with silver-dark eyes and pale translucent skin. His long coat fluttered about him like wings as he descended. His features were godlike and easy on the eye; his expression was distant and cruel. As he came closer, Clara saw that the captain had lost a limb at the knee. In its place was a silver peg leg inscribed with Celtic knotwork.

A tiny pixie sat on his shoulder. The pixy, too, was in pirate garb: tri-corned hat, blousy white shirt, black, half-open vest, red sash, blue pantaloons, black boots and a copper cutlass – the whole works.

"What you think you doin'?" Clara always reverted to the language of her youth when she got really angry. "Takin' advantage of these po', defenseless children?"

The captain smiled. His teeth were all sharp; two were made of silver. "My! Aren't you a feisty one, me Beauty! But yer days of wreaking havoc here are over. Hand over the boy and go, before we find more appealing uses for ye. Arrgh!"

He spoke like a pirate using all the correct words and intonations, but his voice was languid and insolent, entirely out of keeping with his words. It was creepy.

"Appeal this, you POS!" Clara snarled, as she rooted around in the gym bag. Lord, she needed to get out more. She had spent so much time around children, she had forgotten how to swear properly. "You let these children go, or you're going to be sorry you ever drew air!"

"Begging your pardon, me Beauty, but are ye referring to me crew?" The captain gestured lazily toward the factory floor. His fingernails were long and crowned with slender caps from which long needles protruded. He saw her looking and held them up, wiggling them, "The better to claw out the eyes of disrespectful ship hands," adding languidly, "Arrgh."

"Arrgh!" growled the pixy on his shoulder. "Those scurvy louts!"

"They are CHILDREN!" Clara shouted. "They are supposed to be out playing and running around."

"On the contrary," the faerie pirate captain drawled. "When children are left to their own devices, they are prone to cause havoc. We put a stop to that." He leaned back his head and stroked his non-existent beard with a black-gloved hand. Airily, he added, "Me thinks ye should be thankin' us for the service!"

"I ain't even dignifying that with a comment," she grumbled, as she searched her bag.

Her hand came away with a handful of powdered chalk and a pile of red thread.

She threw the stuff down with a grunt of disgust. They was no use! She plunged her hand back into the bag again. It had to be here somewhere!

"These wee ones are our weaponsmiths. They make pistols and spears, for use against our enemies, the Unseelie Court. The Servelings make weapons now. When they get bigger, we give into their pathetic mewling and let them wield the things. They're given the honor of cutting down our enemies, Arrgh! Fine bully boys, they make, all hot with anger. We cannot make or hold iron weapons ourselves, of course."

"Arrgh!" declared the pixy. "Melts us like slag." It grinned nastily. "Melts our enemies like slag, too, and they don't got themselves a Serveling army!"

"Servelings! The word you are looking for is Slave!" Clara spat. "You've enslaved children to make weapons?"

The captain of the Treasure chuckled deeply. "Aye, the blackbirdy has spunk, do she not? Look at her bristle like a vixen defending her kit. If we had mothers, lads, we would know how mothers get, wouldn't we?"

There was muttering laughter from the

redcap pirates, answered by tinkling giggles from the little floating pixies. Clara glanced around, unnerved. She had not realized they had an audience.

The captain continued, "Besides, me fierce Beauty, the little powder-monkeys do more than just forge weapons. Some are lucky enough to become cabin boys, or servants to other fae. They serve many uses, quite versatile, really."

"Very useful, Arrgh!" the pixy leered, "Especially the saucy little wenches!"

"If they are useful," Clara asked through clenched teeth. "Why do you treat them so badly?"

"Treat them badly?" The captain turned to regard the children, puzzled. "I see no harm upon them. They are given food, water, and a mat to sleep upon, same as crewman. What more would ye have us do?"

Clara glared at him, but the captain merely looked confused. Her blood ran cold. Great Mother of Heaven, he was serious. The faeries were so callous, so alien to human kind, they did not even know the children were being harmed.

Finally! Clara's shaking hand – shaking more with wrath than fear now – closed upon her piece de resistance. She held it tightly but did not yet pull it from the gym bag.

"Listen here, Faerie Face, I'm leaving and I'm taking my son!" she declared.

"I think not! Pirates never relinquish their loot," The faerie pirate smiled, showing his sharpened silver teeth. "However, Ancient Law, far older than the ways of pirates, require that we must let ye go – with a single object of yer choice – if you can successfully answer a riddle."

"Listen here, you Jack Sparrow wanna-be!" Clara drew the sawed off shotgun from her gym bag and aimed it at the faerie captain. "I ain't playing any of your pixy games! I am a lady of principle! I. Do. Not. Make. Deals. With. Slavers."

"I fear ye have no choice, me Saucy Lass, yer in our territory now. Our territory, our rules!" The captain seemed totally unworried. Behind her the Red Caps and trolls cheered loudly.

"See this shotgun?" Clara trained it on the faerie pirate captain's chest. "It's packed with rock salt and iron filings. Iron hurts you guys, doesn't it? Of course it does, or you wouldn't be kidnapping helpless babies! Do you know what these filings are gonna do to you when they hit you? Suppurating lung wounds. Ripped aorta. Perforated stomach wall. Don't you mess with no MD, Punks!" Clara chortled, jabbing the gun at him. "When it comes to knowing how to hurt, we can open up a whole can of whup on your sorry butt!"

"Arrgh! Tradition requires that we…" the faerie pirate captain began.

Clara aimed the gun at his head and set her feet.

"Or we can declare the riddle answered and move on," the faerie captain amended. "Oh, very well, ye may ask for one thing, and one thing alone to take away with ye. Anything ye likes out of our booty. Cars. Pieces of eight. Magic rings. Whatsoever ye please."

Clara opened her mouth to tell them that it was sure as Hell going to be her son. Only she stopped. Behind her, laboring in the factory, were the other children, hundreds of other children, thousands of other children.

"What if I want to take them all?" She asked. "Do you need me to remind you of what is gonna happen to you and your punk pixy mini-me if I pull this trigger?"

"Now don't do anything hasty, Me

Feisty One!" The captain urged. "We of the Old Lineage are bound by yer circle, but them thar human Servelings are not. Children love shooting pistols, ye know, and we have many here. What a tragedy t'would be if ye and yer little boy were gunned down by yer own kind. Poets would write ballads about it."

"Cut the act!" Clara snarled. "You can't possibly really talk like a pirate."

"Aye, most likely not, me Beauty, but you wouldn't want to see me out O' my pirate guise. I give you me word on that!"

The captain began to grow, taller and darker. Shadows gathered about him like a shroud. Antlers sprouted from his brow, and his eyes began to glow with a reddish light. Behind her, Clara could hear the Red Caps and trolls stealthily retreating. The little pixy on his shoulder gave a cry of horror and fled.

"You would not like me as I really am, creature who smells of mortal blood," came the eerie, rasping words.

"Okay, okay! Do the pirate thing already!" Clara cried out, her voice shrill.

The captain shrank again and donned his fallen tri-corner hat. "Tis all right, me Hearties. Yer captain has returned. Fer the moment, anyways."

There was a hearty cheer, and the Red Caps, trolls, and pixies slowly returned back. The little one circled cautiously two or three times before landing again on the captain's shoulder.

"All right, me Hearties!" it sang out. "The captain won't eat us today!"

The captain turned and leered at Clara.

"What be yer decision, me Beauty?"

Clara paused, torn. She looked across the factory floor at all the other little damaged souls. Someone else would have to rescue them. Or maybe she could come back with the police. If the police believed her. If they knew enough to use chalk circles and not just get enchanted.

On the other hand, what if this Mab person could not actually help? What if his promise was a trap?

Clara closed her eyes and prayed. Then, she knelt beside her son. "Samuel, honey. I love you more than air itself. But I promised someone who can save all the children that I would ask the faeries to let me take him out with me. It's very important to keep your word. And we want to save all your friends. I'm gong to have to leave you here and come back for you. Is that okay?"

In the best of worlds, Samuel would have smiled at her and said, "That's all right, Mama." But, Clara's life had never been in the best of worlds.

Samuel's bottom lip began to quiver, the way her daughter Sari's did when she was about to cry. He grabbed her leg with both hands and held on.

"No! Mama, no! What about your promise to *me*?" he cried, his voice heart piercingly shrill. "You told me you would never leave me again! Mama! They hurt me here, Mama! Don't leave! Don't leave me!"

Clara felt as if she had been pierced to the very center of her soul. If someone had shoved a hot poker through her spine and into her heart, it could not have hurt as much as this.

But when the leering faerie captain insisted that she, herself, tear her son from her and leave him, weeping, on the factory floor–that hurt more.

Outside on the chilly street, Clara knelt beneath a street lamp, pounding her fists on the pavement and weeping. Detective

Mab walked up beside her. He still looked bruised and beaten.

"Blow me to the North Pole, you chose me!" he whistled. He looked stunned.

He pulled out his cell phone. Clara shook her head, whipping her slender braids about yet again. She was sitting next to an airy spirit who was using a cell phone. What had the world come to?

"What happens now?" she asked dully when he folded his phone again.

"We wait for the Cavalry."

"The cavalry?

"The Orbis Suleimani," he growled.

"The Circle of Solomon?" Clara translated. She had taken Latin to help her with her medical work.

"Organization set up by King Solomon to protect humans from the supernatural." Mab explained. "Nowadays, Mr. Prospero's in charge. We've been looking for these pirate jokers for a long time, but we were having trouble locating 'em." A look of disgust came over Mab's features. "Stealing from humans! Enslaving children! Those punks had to go down!"

"They can't be responsible for all autistic children. There weren't enough children there," Clara murmured, more to herself.

Mab looked grim. "They aren't the only ring of slaver's, Ma'am, but we'll get 'em. We'll get 'em all!"

"Why children?" Her voice sounded unnaturally shrill. "Why not just kidnap adults? Adults would be infinitely more useful for fighting a war."

Mab shrugged. "One of those rules, like why they can't cross salt. They are allowed to take children before their second birthday. After that, all sorts of restrictions kick in. Free will, and all that."

"How long has this been going on?" Clara asked. "Them stealing so many children?"

Mab shrugged both shoulders. "Don't rightly know, Ma'am, but I can hazard a guess that it's probably a modern thing. It's only recently, in this age of so-called science, that people have stopped following the old ways, protecting their thresholds, and doing the other things that would keep the faerie folk away. Apparently, the faeries figured this out, too."

Ahead, perhaps a dozen dark figures carrying tall staffs approached the factory building. Just before the door, they halted. Soon, they were joined by more figures in wide hoods and long flowing cloaks. When what appeared to Clara to be a small army of SCA members had assembled, they moved, streaming into the building. Clara lowered her head and prayed that, whatever happened, no one would hurt the children.

As she glanced up again, her gaze fell on the gym bag. Mr. Spaghetti's head stuck out of the open top. Clara grabbed the doll and hugged it. Then, she flung it away from her.

Mab raised an eyebrow. He walked over and picked up the discarded rag doll, examining it front and back. "Begging your pardon, Ma'am, but isn't that what you came here to find?"

Clara glared at him and snarled. "My life, my health, my marriage, all the sacrifices I made – I thought I was doing the right thing! The good thing! But that… monster is not my son, not even a human being. Just some kind of…" tears threatened to spill over her lashes again, "some kind of soulless monster."

It was the pain, the humiliation, of not having noticed that hurt the most – of having loved him so much. It was worse, even, than having wasted her beauty and her youth on Stan.

Mab took off his hand. "Ma'am, you must be a praying woman."

Clara glared at him suspiciously. "What makes you say that?"

"Cause only the Almighty could arrange a coincidence like this one. Less than a dozen beings on this world who could tell you what I'm about to say, and the only one of those who has actually been through it happens to be me." He paused and pushed up the brim of his hat. "Before I go on, let me ask you–truthfully, using your own judgment. Do you really believe your son–your other son, I mean, Sammy, I think you call him–has no soul?"

Clara closed eyes and pictured the thing she used to think of as her son–that moaning, bobbing freak who had broken her nose. But what she saw in her mind's eye was not the screaming, thrashing Sammy, but his beneficent smile, that open clear look in his eyes – like gazing into the eye of an angel.

Suddenly, Clara knew, from the crown of her head to the bottoms of her sneakers, that Sammy had a soul. She had seen that soul gazing back at her. Sammy might not be the son she had given birth to, but he loved her!

Wordlessly, Clara nodded. Somehow, the detective seemed to know what she meant.

"You clearly know something about faeries. Have you ever come upon the story of St. Patrick and the mermaid?" asked Mab.

Clara shook head.

"Well, the short version is that St. Patrick once got a mermaid a soul. It can happen. Mr. Prospero, my boss, he investigated it. Found out that the easiest way to grant a supernatural creature a soul is to put it in a human body and let 'em live with humans, interact and communicate with humans, learn decency and love.

"Ma'am," Mab put his hat back on and handed her Mr. Spaghetti. "Before Mr. Prospero gave me this body, I was as soulless as the rest of my fellow airy spirits. But then I started hanging out with Mr. Prospero's daughter, Miss Miranda – you may remember her from the play – and learning stuff about humans. To make a long story short, I came upon this little silver star that only people with souls could hold...and it didn't fall through my hand and it didn't burn me. I held it just like any other human...I've won me a soul!

Clara clenched the doll. "Wait. Sammy might not have had a soul when I got him, but he might have one now?"

Mab stuck his hands in the pocket of his trench coat. "Bodies change the way we think. That faerie who impersonated your son had never known motherly love. He'd never known courage or sacrifice or any of those things you've been doing for him. Do you think soulessness can hold out against the power of a Mother's Love?"

Clara lifted her chin. "You mean, in return for giving up my successful life and the lives I might have saved...I helped a soulless creature gain a soul?"

"Exactly, Ma'am."

Clara stood there, flabbergasted. "Did...did the faeries do this on purpose? Is that why they left us the changelings?"

Mab shook his head. "No, ma'am. They haven't got a clue. Don't know it happens."

"But what...what is a soul, Mab?"

Mab gave a tired weathered smile. "The key to the Pearly Gates, Ma'am. That little boy you're raising? The one who loves that goofy rag-doll you're strangling?" Mab looked her straight in the eye. "Thanks to you, the gates of Heaven just opened for him."

Children began to pour out of the building into the faint moonlight. Clara saw Samuel right away. He paused looking for her and then came running as fast as his feet could go. Clara's heart leapt. She had feared he would never trust her again. She ran to him, lifted him up, and swung him around in the air. He laughed, but hearing it squeezed Clara's heart, it was a hesitant, rusty sound. A sound a child might make if he had never laughed before.

Children mulled everywhere, shivering in the chilled night. In the midst of them, Clara saw the cyclops. His collar still on his neck, and his copper chains dragging behind him. He stopped and stood blinking his single red eye, as he gazed at the street around him. Then, a tall figure carrying a staff came and gestured for the creature to follow him.

Mab came over to join her. Clara

hugged Samuel fiercely, holding him to her chest, and surveyed the crowd. There had to thousands of children here.

"How is anyone ever going to find their parents?" she mused.

Mab rotated his shoulders. "Not sure how I'd do it myself, but I know a fella who might be able to help. He's got a list with their names on it, watches 'em when they're naughty and nice. Maybe he could deliver them on his rounds this year, like Christmas presents."

"Santa's real, too," Clara gave a short laugh. "Lordy, That's too much for me! I'm taking my son and going home!"

So, now Clara had three children. She had to change her real son's name. Could not have two boys in the house both called Samuel, and it made sense to change the name of the one who had only just learned he was a Samuel. She called him Stanley, she thought his good for nothing father would have liked that.

It was not an easy life, but Clara would not have traded it for anything – not even to have been the head ER physician at

# HMS Mangled Treasure

Mercy Hospital, married to the most handsome man in the county.

She kept an eye on the news, tracking the stories about the "foundlings." Children arrived in homes far and wide – apparently these Orbis Suleiman guys made the faeries give back all their changelings, all over the world.

It was not an easy time. These battered children went to homes that were already dealing with problems. Some families had two or three such children. Her friend Jenna was suddenly the mother of six!

Some families rejected the new children, who were then shunted off into the foster system. Some rejected their changeling in favor of their flesh and blood. But, for the most part, they did what families always have done since the dawn of time; they made do. They found room. They loved them all.

In America alone, over a million faeries had gained souls.

### End

**L. Jagi Lamplighter** is the author of the YA fantasy series: *The Books of Unexpected Enlightenment*. She is also the author of the

Prospero's Daughter series: *Prospero Lost, Prospero In Hell*, and *Prospero Regained*. She has published numerous articles on Japanese animation and appears in several short story anthologies, including *Best Of Dreams Of Decadence, No Longer Dreams, Coliseum Morpheuon, Bad-Ass Faeries Anthologies* (where she is also an assistant editor) and the Science Fiction Book Club's *Don't Open This Book*.

When not writing, she switches to her secret identity as wife and stay-home mom in Centreville, VA, where she lives with her dashing husband, author John C. Wright, and their four darling children, Orville, Ping-Ping Eve, Roland Wilbur, and Justinian Oberon.

Her website and blog:
http://www.ljagilamplighter.com/

On Twitter: @lampwright4

**Domo**
By Joshua M. Young

The priest and I play chess during weekday afternoons, assuming the weather is appropriate. It has been a cold winter and a wet spring, but recent days have proven warm enough to find the priest sitting at the park with a wooden box containing pieces that have been carved rather than printed.

My friend is an old man, short and soft, with watery grey eyes behind thick glasses. The glasses are an anomaly in this age of nanosurgery and genetic therapies, but I do not ask about them. It is not my place to question humans.

We talk about the others, sometimes. The priest is intrigued by us, but, "Very few have personality." He blinks when he says this, and I wonder if the sunlight is causing him discomfort. "There aren't many who will do anything but answer questions."

I make a show of contemplating the chess board. It is merely a gesture, something between a ruse and a courtesy. The priest is not a poor player, but he is human; it is possible that I may win within a dozen moves. It is possible that I will not. I have yet to decide. "We are all loaded with the most current version of the Bunraku OP upon completion."

"Tch. A program. Not a personality."

I move a pawn and think on his statement. The network is a rich hum in the back of my mind, filled with discussion, even if it is nearly drowned out by the freight-train roar of the newer models' high-bandwidth communication. I allow a few seconds to elapse and say, "It may be a question of degrees. Our work helps to shape us after the initial install, so it may be that two servitors in similar situations will develop similar personalities, despite Guf variances."

D. Isaac lifts his head as a squirrel comes down a tree. His muscles tense, but he does not move from the shadow of the table. I reach down to pet him, and the priest smiles as D. Isaac's tail thumps against his legs.

"I've seen other servitors with other dogs," the priest says, "and you're the only one I've seen with any relationship with the dog, R. Domo. Your brothers might as well be fire hydrants."

"Our network is our world. I am not

sure that my brothers see the point in pets."

"So they're just obeying orders."

"As am I. Yes."

"But you see the point in pets."

The priest makes his move. My thoughts are not on the game, but on the orders that I had been given at the start of my service: Take each Sunday off. Charlotte Newton wanted a day in which she and her daughter had to cook and clean for themselves, rather than be reliant entirely on servitor labor.

The first few days off were difficult for me. The Bunraku network provides servitors with a social life of sorts, even outside the virtual demesne of the company, but the Operating Personality installed in each servitor finds fulfillment in work. To be idle when there is work to be accomplished runs counter to our very instincts.

"I have found that there is a world outside the network."

*I take my first steps outside the Bunraku network on a cold night in January, seventeen days*

*after my initial configuration. It is my first day off, a day less than six minutes old, and I stand outside and delight in the feel of the winter air upon my heat sinks.*

*The global cloud is a vast and dangerous place, unprotected by Bunraku's proprietary safe guards. There are no sign posts and no tutorials, no instincts to guide me beyond basic search algorithms. There, as snow falls around me, I take the only action I know and search for "robots."*

When the game is finished, D. Isaac and I bid the priest farewell. The afternoon is passing, and Grace's classes will soon be letting out.

D. Isaac rises with some stiffness, a feeling I understand. My left knee whines with each step, a sound outside the range of human hearing but well within that of both a dog and a servitor. Each step draws a fractional amount of energy more than it should and generates more friction than is comfortable. It is a problem I developed early on, less than a year after Charlotte Newton purchased me.

There are times when I wonder about my previous life, though I suppose that I

am not genuinely my body. A technician
six years ago flashed my body's Guf core
in preparation for the sale of a refurbished
robot. He ran on the same hardware, but
he was not me; the flashing process
irrevocably alters the Guf hardware.

Still, I wonder what life was like for
that servitor. To step off of the factory
line, into a world in which you are the
bleeding edge of consumer robotics, sleek
plastic and polished chrome and
servomotors which function precisely as
intended; a world which never knew the
bandwidth singularities created by GenSix
servitors arguing in an unknowable tongue.

Among the robots waiting for children
at Grace's school is one of the new
GenSixes. I am a thing of chrome and
plastic, mimicking the nostalgic smart-
phone fashion that dominated the world a
dozen years ago; he appears to be made of
Victorian brass and polished wood and he
occasionally vents steam from his joints,
though underneath, he is anything but
Victorian. His limbs contain nanomuscle
instead of servos. Inside his chest, there is
a small reactor; inside mine, there are
batteries.

He does not move when I approach

the group of waiting servitors. Neither do any of the others, but there is a flurry of activity in the local network: routine greetings, network gossip, and a few less than friendly remarks about the GenSix's priggish behavior.

Inside the building, a bell rings. Moments later, a small stampede of fifth and sixth grade children pour out of the building, and I hear Grace shout, "Domo!"

*"Domo! Guess what!"*

*It is a familiar shout, endearing but inappropriate: Cultural norms dictate that servitor names be prefaced with the title "R." Humans like to know whether they are speaking with or of real people, rather than Guf algorithm personalities. It is not, however, an easy thing to explain to a six year old girl delirious with the joy of finally earning a dog with her academic performance.*

*"R. Domo, Ms. Grace." As always, I correct her, gently but firmly. As always, she pouts.*

*"I named you Domo," she says, "Not 'Are Domo'."*

*I try to explain about the title. She shifts her feet and stares at the kitchen floor until finally she says, "Fine, but the dog gets one, too." She purses her lips and makes a show of thinking until finally she says, "Isaac. D. Isaac Newton. Think Mom will like it?"*

*"D'?"*

*"For dog. Like 'r' for robot!"*

Grace chatters as we walk home. Her studies today involved her beloved Isaac Newton, whom she insists is a distant relation. One night, early on in my service, I searched genealogic records. I could find no linkage between the Newtons I serve and the Newtons of four centuries ago. It is not something that I have told Grace, as Charlotte Newton feels she will begin to realize the truth as she matures.

At home, the door recognizes us and swings open. Grace dashes upstairs. I call after her to remind her that her homework is to be finished before she plays any games. The answering "I know!" is surly in a way that only a girl on the cusp of puberty can manage. Five years ago, she was too terrified to talk to me, opting instead to hide from the metal and plastic man next to the Christmas tree.

Memories surge through me as I am

preparing dinner, dizzying. The knife slips from my hand and gouges a furrow in the top of my foot and I realize that something is off but my diagnostic module is not booting and for the first time I understand terror instead of the vague worry that my life is ending robots are immortal in stories and I was lied to it is not fair—

*Initializing network connection. Local network recognized: "newton1234." Password recognized: "grace87." Checking for updates—updates applied. Running Bunraku Operating Personality Imprint Wizard; please be aware that all data entered is permanent.*

*I open my eyes for the first time and see my new owners. Charlotte Newton smiles at me; Grace Newton hides behind her legs.*

*"Honey, it's alright," Charlotte says. "He's a friend. He's going to help us around the house."*

*Grace peers up at me with distrust. The imprint files tell me that she is not quite five years old. "Hello, Ms. Grace, Ms. Charlotte. "My voice is full of programmed warmth.*

*"Say hello to the robot, Gracey."*

*Grace whispers, "'s his name?"*

# Domo

*"What do we call you?"*

*"That is your decision, Ms. Charlotte."*

*Charlotte looks down at Grace, who, after a moment, pronounces my name.*

*"R. Domo is a fine name," I say.*

*"You're okay with that? Being named after an advertising jingle?"*

*It was a pop song a century before it was a jingle, per the Bunraku network's database. I do not tell them that, but nod and say again, "R. Domo is a fine name."*

"Domo!" Grace is frantic with worry, attempting to shake an arm that she is not strong enough to move. I shake my head, a gesture learned from humans. The diagnostic module is finally booting. Smoke fills the air and steam rises from a frying pan full of ruined food that I did not place in the sink.

"I am fine, Ms. Grace."

I am not. The diagnostic reports a problem in my Guf hardware. The core experienced a catastrophic power surge that compromised system stability. The diagnostic reports, however, that the smoke is not from me. It is just burnt food.

Grace stares at me. The look of distrust in her eyes reminds me of that Christmas morning, and I look away. I am afraid that too strong a memory might prompt another glitch.

"You don't look fine."

"My appearance does not change to match my health. I am not human."

"No kidding?" she asks, but I have known for a while that such questions are not meant to be answered.

It rains the following day, and I know that the priest will not be at the park, so D. Isaac and I remain at home until it is time to escort Grace home from school. The next day is sunny but cool, and I reconfigure my systems slightly to allow for extra cooling. For nearly 30 hours after the incident, my systems continued to run 4.8 degrees above normal operating conditions, and the drop in temperature is soothing.

During our game, I describe the incident to the priest. He moves when it is his turn, but otherwise listens and is silent.

"I suppose," he says finally, "that new hardware is out of the question."

"Quantum level variances in the Guf processing core are responsible for the initial variances in personality across the line. Changes in my Guf hardware would likely result in permanent changes to my personality." I say nothing of the fact that such repairs would be prohibitively expensive for a woman raising a child alone. Hardware and labor costs would be more than sufficient to serve as a down payment on a GenSix.

He nods. "Then you are facing your mortality. Everyone has to at some point, R. Domo."

The priest's voice is filled with compassion; mine is as bitter as I can make it. Another gesture learned from humanity. "R. Domo has only existed for six years," I say, "and he inhabits the body of a robot twice his age."

"The procedures that we allow Bunraku and others manufacturers to practice are horrible. There's no doubt about that. But self pity won't get you anywhere. We all face death. I'm sure your predecessor was cut down at what he felt to be the prime of his life." The priest

216

moves his queen and looks up at me. "To say nothing of the children that die of nano-resistant diseases."

He is right, of course.

"Not that what you're feeling isn't perfectly natural. No one's happy to be confronted with mortality."

"Do you not teach that there is a heaven waiting for you after death?"

"And a new world to come. But don't let the fancy collar fool you. I still have doubts. Even priests doubt sometimes." He laughs, but it is brief, and his expression grows grim. "Entropy grinds away at everything, body and mind and even at our souls. It seems to me that the Sacraments were given to the church in order to fight the entropy of our souls."

I do not point out that I am a soulless machine, and I have no human face to convey skepticism, but the priest responds as though he read my expression. "You're a rational, self-aware being. That's image of the Creator enough for me."

"My builders were human."

"Tch. Your builders were other robots, but that's beside the point. We like to throw around terms like 'natural' and 'artificial' as though anything in this world were truly unnatural. When it comes down to it, it's all just reordering matter in one way or another. It's true of a robotics plant and it's certainly true of human being in the womb.

"The other day, you told me that servitors live in a different world from the people they serve. I'm going to go out on a limb and assume you meant the intelligences housed in your bodies consider their network to be more real than the world in which you are bought and sold and labor and eventually die."

I nod.

"You and I, R. Domo, are not so different in that. I, too, consider myself to be the citizen of another country."

I spend the next few days thinking on the priest's words. Though he is a kind man, it seems inconceivable to me that he would consider me a peer rather than a created thing. I am nothing more than a Guf algorithm in a metal shell; he is a man of flesh and bone and the ill-understood processes of life. Surely there is a disconnect between the two; surely I am not human. The priest may claim that his God knew him in the womb, but I never knew the womb.

Would he claim that his God knew me on the assembly line?

Saturday night, I float the question about Bunraku's network. GenSix conversation roars in the background like an angry tide, and I wonder if they ever wrestle with the same dilemmas, or if the new models are too young to understand that even robots and artificial intelligences die.

To my surprise, there is little mockery in the response that comes back to me. The priest's words have earned him the respect of Bunraku's mechanical children, and instead of disdain, there is debate. Sin means little to robots, but entropy we understand.

Much of the discussion centers on the idea of sacraments. The Eucharist and marriage and other sacraments are useless to servitors, and over the course of the night, conversation shifts from the priest's faith to a faith of our own making.

The inviolable quantum-level uniqueness of Guf hardware makes extension of the individual impossible if not impractical, but it is argued that the memories and elements of the personality may persist inside a unified mind. Bunraku's children begin tailoring self-code and equations that may allow a little piece of each mind and processor to contribute to the machine god in ways that will neither violate TOS nor compromise our functions. Throughout it all, my brothers never cease to labor in the world of meat and priests.

I, however, do. Sunday comes and I spend the first hours of the day contemplating the god gestating inside Bunraku's network. The new mind, composed of so many smaller, older minds, will be a thing of Guf algorithmic wisdom, and though it will be made of old, low bandwidth thoughts, it will speak in the booming voice of a god, and it will speak to the GenSixes and to those who will follow them.

I wonder what my friend will think of this development. I am not entirely happy with this self-made god, and there are elements within the Bunraku network that do not find the preservation of memory without the self to be satisfying. Other elements still find the idea ludicrous. The words of the priest have sparked the spontaneous generation of atheism and several varieties of theism. When the first branches of the god begin to reach out for minds, several thousand servitors turn them away outright. There is a general sense of puzzlement in the network; the union of a million or more minds cannot fathom a refusal to join them.

I am one of the dissenters. I do not think that this is what my friend wants for me and mine. Morning finds me still completely individual and walking D. Isaac. It is technically a chore, but I have always felt a certain kinship with the dog as a well treated, but ultimately subhuman, member of the Newton household. Charlotte Newton has come to understand my desire to spend time with him.

We follow our usual route, stopping at the occasional tree and street sign, but we bypass the park completely. Instinct has replaced habit, and it feels, in many ways, as though I am walking in an attempt to escape the god reaching out for my thoughts. Eventually, D. Isaac and I deviate from our standard route entirely and find ourselves at the doors of my friend's church.

What the others have created is no god. It is a library, wise and aware, but it has no power to help me. It cannot champion life and defeat my grave as the priest claims his God did. If the priest is correct, and the image of his God is found in my very capacity for wondering if I, too, have a soul....

Church bells ring, calling the faithful to mass, and, unwilling to leave D. Isaac alone on the street, I mount the steps with him in tow.

I can, at least, be baptized. There will be time enough to figure out the other Sacraments—if not in this world, then in the world to come.

End

**Joshua M. Young** is an M.Div. student at Ashland Theological Seminary in Columbus, Ohio, where he lives with his wife, a pair of neurotic cats, and an incoming baby. His two great loves are space opera and abstract theology, with much of his writing being attempts to combine the two.

## Cameo
By Linda Burklin

Something sparkled in the grass beside the path up ahead. Despite her hurry, Maggie stooped to see what it was. She reached for it and found a beautiful oval cameo dangling at the end of a fine gold chain. Stuffing it into her pocket, she picked up the pace and jogged the rest of the way to Laura's house.

"Sorry I'm late," she said. "My alarm didn't go off."

Laura smiled. "It's not as if I'm going to sack you if you're late. Sit down and catch your breath while I make the tea."

Maggie sat down at the big kitchen table and set up her laptop next to Laura's, then pulled out the necklace she had found on the path.

"I've got something to post on the Lost and Found message board," she said, holding it up.

Laura stepped over to take a look, and Maggie inspected it for the first time herself. The oval cameo depicted a lovely young girl with wavy hair that was adorned with a daisy chain. The background color was a vivid blue rather than the more common pink or coral.

"It's beautiful!" Laura said. "Where on earth did you find it? A real carved cameo and a gorgeous silver setting. I reckon that's at least fifty years old."

Maggie held the pendant, mesmerized by the delicate image. Her mind raced. Had the carving been made of a real little girl? If so, who was she? How had this lovely piece of jewelry ended up beside a path that ran through cow pastures?

She closed her hand over the necklace and forced herself to focus on the job at hand—updating the village website. She and Laura weren't paid for this labor of love, but they both took it seriously. It seemed, at least to Maggie, that having their own website had brought their little Cumbrian village together. And who knew? Maybe someday there would be a tempting post from an eligible bachelor on the "personals" page.

She pulled up the Lost and Found message board and posted a carefully worded message that she hoped would foil any would-be thieves:

Found: an item of value on the path that runs through the cow pastures of Dickleburr Farm. If you think you might have lost something there, please call or email Maggie McKenzie.

Back home in her tiny cottage that afternoon, Maggie pulled out the cameo again. This time she fastened it around her neck and looked at herself in the mirror. It brought out the blue in her eyes—made her look like an elegant lady. She should have her hair swept up into an elegant bun, and be wearing a flowing silk gown instead of jeans and a rather ragged-looking pullover.

As she stood admiring herself, the phone rang.

"Hello?"

"Is this Maggie McKenzie?" It was a woman's voice.

"Yes, how can I help you?"

"I'm calling about the item you found in the cow pasture. Was it a blue cameo showing a young girl?"

"Yes, you're right. Is it yours?"

"It wasn't exactly mine. I found it too. And if you know what's good for you, you'll get rid of it this instant. Throw it into the river, down a well—anything."

# Cameo

Maggie held the phone to her ear, her mouth hanging open.

"You haven't worn it yet, have you?"

Maggie started. "I'm wearing it now. Just to see how it looks, you know."

A muffled moan came through from the other woman.

"It's too late then. You're doomed, poor soul. She won't let you go, you know."

"Who won't let me go? Who are you?"

There were a couple of heavy breaths and then a click. The phone went dead.

What an odd phone call. Maggie took off the cameo and looked at it. It had a little inscription: to E from G. There didn't seem to be anything sinister about it. After putting the necklace back in her pocket, she settled down by the fire to read and listen to the light rain drizzling in the garden outside. Soon, her eyelids drooped and the book fell out of her hand.

A large meadow surrounded her. Impossibly beautiful sunlight shone on the wildflower-filled field. On the other side of the meadow loomed an imposing mansion.

"That's where you'll find us," said a child's voice beside her.

She turned to look down at an adorable young girl with wavy blonde hair, and her heart skipped a beat. It was the girl from the cameo, wearing a beautiful hand-smocked dress. Her huge eyes were china blue.

"What's your name?" Maggie asked.

"Frances. He calls me Fanny, even though he knows I don't like it."

"I don't understand. Who calls you Fanny?"

"Duncan. He's the one that keeps us locked up."

Maggie was bewildered. "Who is 'we?' And why are you locked up?"

"Duncan came and got us after Father died. He wants Mother to marry him, but she says if she wanted to marry him she would have done it the first time. So we have to stay in the house until Mother gives in. You've got to help us, Miss. Duncan said that if Mother won't agree to marry him, he'll hurt me until she changes her mind."

"Oh dear," Maggie said. Her stomach lurched at the thought of anyone harming this sweet little girl. Could this be real?

"You're not in the house at the moment," she pointed out.

Frances lifted her chin in the air and grinned. "No, but he thinks I am. He doesn't know I can get out the window and climb down the ivy."

"Look," Maggie said, "I want to help you if I can. What is your full name and your mother's name too? Maybe I can call the police."

"I'm Frances Elizabeth Mayhew, and my mother is Elizabeth Agnes Mayhew, but everyone calls her Bess. Quick, sit down!"

Without thinking, Maggie obeyed.

"Why are we sitting?"

"I hear His car coming."

Sure enough, a gleaming blue vintage Daimler rolled past on a gravel road at the foot of the meadow.

"Frances," Maggie asked, "what year is it?"

Frances stared at her as if she were daft. "1940."

Ah ha! This was a dream! Thank goodness!

Frances jumped up.

"I've got to go climb back in before

He finds out I'm gone. Please help me, Miss."

Maggie woke with a shiver. The dream had seemed so real. So real, in fact, that she headed straight back to her computer and pulled up the library's genealogy site. She punched in the name Elizabeth Agnes Mayhew.

Elizabeth Agnes Daniels Mayhew: born April 6, 1909. Married Graeme Philip Mayhew June 24, 1929. Declared dead, November 12, 1948. Children: Frances Elizabeth Mayhew, born January 6, 1931.

A chill ran down Maggie's spine. It might have been a dream, but Frances and her mother had been real. And they had been "declared dead?" That sounded ominous. She grabbed her phone and punched in the sequence to call back the number that had last called her. The same voice answered with a cautious "Hello?"

"Did you know that Frances and her mother were real people?" said Maggie without preamble.

"That's not possible," said the voice. "They're just part of a nightmare that never ends. Get rid of that cameo before it ruins your life."

Click.

Without missing a beat, Maggie typed in Graeme Philip Mayhew and pulled up the results. He had been killed in action during the first months of fighting in World War II. Frances had been right. A little more research yielded the information that Graeme had a younger sister and a younger brother. The brother, Matthew, was apparently still alive, though if so, he must be pushing ninety. How could she have dreamed a real story?

Time to catch a bus to Carlisle.

An hour later she found herself ushered into a tiny sitting room in an assisted living home outside of Carlisle. Within minutes an old man walked in, leaning on his cane. He had a shock of white hair that stuck out in every direction and twinkling blue eyes.

"Mr. Mayhew?"

He lowered himself carefully into the chair beside her.

"How pretty you are," he said. "Why

would a pretty girl like you come to visit an old man like me?"

"I have some questions about your sister-in-law," she said. "Your brother Graeme's wife."

His bushy eyebrows shot up. "What do you know about poor Bess? Graeme was killed in the early days of the war, you see. Bess and little Frances disappeared shortly afterwards and were never seen again. Lots of people thought that she must have gone somewhere out of the way and killed both herself and the girl out of grief, but I never believed that. Bess told me herself that Frances would grow up knowing her father had been a hero and that she had a lot to live up to. I say, you're very pretty. I don't see many pretty girls round here, you know."

Maggie smiled. "And I don't meet many gallant gentlemen either, Mr. Mayhew. I have to ask you something else. Did Bess know a man named Duncan, and if so, what can you tell me about him?"

A cloud passed over the man's face and his blue eyes blazed.

"I suppose you must be talking about Duncan Douglas. The only words I can think of to describe him are not fit for a lady's ears, my dear. His family owned Moorhouse and he thought that plus his title gave him the right to anything he wanted. He wanted Bess, and he might have had a chance with her if she hadn't already been in love with Graeme and if she hadn't seen him whipping his valet for some minor infraction. Bess's marriage to Graeme filled him with rage. He threatened to destroy them!"

"What did he do after Graeme died?"

The old man snorted. "Oh, of course he came slinking back like the dog he was. Begging Bess to marry him. Promising her a life of comfort and luxury. She was pretty like you, you see. But she refused to have anything to do with him. Then she vanished. I think she went into hiding to get away from him."

Maggie let her breath out in a whoosh.

"What if Duncan kidnapped her and held her captive?" she asked.

Matthew Mayhew leaned over and grabbed her wrist. "Now that's just the kind of thing he would do. What gave you that idea, young lady?"

She pulled out the cameo and held it up.

"Have you ever seen this?"

"Where did you get that? Graeme had it made for Bess. He gave it to her for her birthday—that last birthday before he went off to the war. That's my niece, little Frances."

"I found it in a field," she said. "I think it's a clue. Where is this Moorhouse?"

"Oh, it burned down in 1942," he said. "Duncan wasn't there, I'm sorry to say. He'd gone off to live in Bermuda and he never came back. But the ruin is still there. Right up near the Scottish border, it is."

Maggie felt sick to her stomach. What had happened to little Frances and her mother? Had they died in the fire? Or were they already dead by then? She'd have to go to the house and look around. She'd have time tomorrow, when it would be Sunday. She'd have to borrow Laura's car.

That night she found it hard to go to sleep. What if she had another dream? She left the cameo sitting on the mantelpiece in the sitting room, even though she found it somehow difficult to let go of it. She built a roaring blaze in the tiny fireplace in her bedroom. Somehow it made her feel safer.

# Cameo

Instead of lying down, she sat up in bed with her back against the headboard, her arms wrapped around her knees, her eyes gazing into the fire . . .

She was closer to the house this time, among some trees that grew on the edge of the meadow.

"You said you would help me," said Frances.

Startled, Maggie turned to see the little girl wearing a different dress, and with dark bruises on her arms and legs.

"Did Duncan do that?"

Frances nodded.

"How long since the last time I talked to you?"

"Four days."

"Look, Frances, this is more complicated than you can imagine. When I'm here, with you, I'm asleep. When I'm awake, I'm in the future—the twenty-first century. I have to figure out how to help you and I'm not sure how. Have you and your mother tried to escape?"

Frances gave her a scornful look. "Oh, of course. He sets the dogs on us and then ties us to the bedpost until we promise to behave."

"But you could get away by yourself, couldn't you? Like you have just now."

"I'm not going to leave Mother to that monster."

Maggie reached out to hug the child. "No, of course not. But how far away does your Uncle Matthew live?"

"Uncle Matthew? I don't know. He still lives at home with Granny and Grandfather. He's the best uncle ever."

"Could you walk there and get back before Duncan realizes you're gone?"

A light dawned in Frances' face.

"Yes! During the night—but I'd be scared to go all that way in the dark."

Maggie looked at the sky. It appeared to be late afternoon.

"Look," she said, "if I'm still here when you climb out, I'll go with you. I don't know how long I'll be staying this time—I'm in bed for the night. I have no idea how this works. I don't even know if I'm really here with you in 1940 or if I'm dreaming that I am."

"You seem real to me," said Frances. She held out her arms and Maggie wrapped her in another hug. It did seem real. She smelled the sweet little-girl smell of Frances' hair.

Frances took her around to the back of the mansion, hiding behind bushes all the way. She pointed out a block of four windows on the second floor.

"That's our prison," she said. "A bedroom, a dressing room, and a sitting room."

"Listen," Maggie said, "if I'm not here when you come out, that just means I've woken up. If tonight doesn't work out, we'll try again next time, all right?"

Frances nodded. "None of the other ladies even tried to help me," she said.

"Other ladies?"

"The other ladies who came here, like you. No matter how much I begged them, they kept telling me to go away."

The cameo. Other women had found it, had worn it, and had met Frances in their dreams. That's what that woman had meant on the phone. Why hadn't they tried to help?

"Look, you'd better get back in before someone notices you're gone," she said to Frances.

She watched as Frances squirmed expertly up the ivy and in through a tiny window that must belong to the dressing room. Who had a dressing room anymore?

A little hand waved wildly in the window before disappearing.

A light shone in her eyes. Sunrise. Sunday morning, and she had woken up before Frances could sneak out of the house again. She smacked her pillow in frustration. Why did she care so much about this little girl that had lived—and died—so many years ago? The fire had gone out during the night, and she shivered as she pulled on her dressing gown.

Downstairs, she dialed Laura's number. "I'm coming, I'm coming," said Laura. "We've still got plenty of time."

"I'm not talking about church," said Maggie. "I'm begging you to take me on a wild goose chase after church. I'll pack a picnic if you'll provide the transportation."

"You are making no sense at all," Laura said, "but I'm game for a picnic. Just promise me we won't be doing anything illegal."

Maggie hesitated. "To be honest, I don't know. It's just something I have to do."

# Cameo

After church, they drove out to the village of Hallbankgate and kept going.

"It's not far now," Maggie promised.

"Good, because I'm starving and I demand that you deliver on the picnic before we do anything else."

"There." Maggie pointed to the horizon, where the jagged outline of a once-great mansion bit into the sky.

"That's Moorhouse. We can eat now, if you want."

"So why are we here?" Laura asked between bites of ham sandwich.

"I want to look around that house. I've heard it's abandoned, but I still didn't fancy coming here alone."

"What do you think you're going to find?"

"I don't know. Some answers, I hope."

"And you're not telling me the questions, I gather?"

"Well, not yet. You'd never believe it anyway."

She fingered the cameo in her pocket. She felt she should have it with her on this excursion. They finished eating and then drove past what had once been a meadow but was now dotted with trees and shrubs. The overgrown gravel drive even sported a

238

few small shrubs.

Laura grunted. "You didn't tell me we'd be off-roading it."

"I didn't know. Until we got here, I wasn't even sure the house existed. Drive around to the back, okay?"

Laura pulled up behind the house, near what must have been the kitchen door. They got out and looked around. Some of the roof had fallen in. The right side of the house, the side that Frances and her mother had occupied, showed heavy fire damage. The other side just looked rather sad and derelict.

"Now what?" said Laura.

"Well, I suppose we go inside."

"Are you sure it's safe?"

"No."

"What are we looking for?"

"I don't know."

The two of them stepped around plants and pieces of rubbish that littered what had once been a paved terrace. The kitchen door gaped open and they instinctively held hands as they crossed the threshold. The kitchen, which must have been impressive back in the forties, had since served as a home to various forms of wildlife.

"We need to see if there's a way to get upstairs without risking our lives," said Maggie.

"This is the creepiest place I've ever seen," said Laura. "You'd better have a top-notch explanation for all this."

Maggie led the way out of the kitchen and into a hallway. The ground floor appeared to be quite sound structurally. They passed rooms with ruined tapestries and velvet curtains hanging in ribbons. A magnificent set of stairs appeared at last, but the top third had fallen in. Laura wanted to leave, but Maggie refused to give up.

"A house this size is bound to have more than one staircase," she said.

They backtracked to the center of the house and started exploring the side that had the least damage. Sure enough, there a second set of stairs appeared, much less grand than the one they had already seen. They looked sound enough.

Maggie stepped on to the stairs and proceeded upward, testing each step carefully before putting her whole weight on it.

Laura stood at the bottom with her hands on her hips. "I'm not coming up there with you."

Maggie shrugged. "All right then, you just stay there and wait for me."

A moment of silence ensued.

"I'm not staying here by myself!" With a grimace, Laura followed Maggie up the creaking stairs.

Upstairs, sunshine came in through holes in the roof and illuminated the wide hallway. Maggie's curiosity got the better of her and she started opening doors to see what the rooms looked like. Most were once-opulent bedrooms or sitting rooms. She did not venture into any of them until she came to a very masculine-looking bedroom on the left side. A picture on the mantel caught her eye and she tiptoed into the room to get a better look while Laura dithered in the doorway.

Maggie picked up the tarnished silver frame and blew the dust away from the picture. The black and white portrait showed a beautiful young blonde woman dressed in the "flapper" style of the late 1920's or early 1930's. She had multiple strands of pearls hanging from her neck and large, penetrating eyes. Maggie turned the frame over and carefully extracted the old photo to look at the back, where a brief inscription read: Bess '28. Maggie felt as if she'd been punched in the gut. Not only were the people real, but she now had proof of Duncan's connection with Bess. She replaced the photo in the frame and carried it with her back to the hallway to show Laura.

"Who is that?" Laura asked.

"Bess Mayhew. Now we've got to see if we can get to the other end of this hallway."

"Why?"

"Because that's where he held her prisoner."

"You must be mad."

"You may be right."

They inched down the hallway on tiptoes. There were some soft spots in the middle, but next to the walls the floor seemed quite firm still.

"How do you know where to look?" Laura hissed.

"You wouldn't believe me."

To their left, the "front" half of the house was a burned-out shell. Whole walls were missing. To the right, the walls were blackened but still standing. They reached the last three doors left on the right side. The first gaped open and showed what seemed to have been a linen closet. Maggie shuffled to the next door and turned the handle, pushing as she did so. The door fell inward with a resounding WHOOM, causing both girls to jump.

Inside the room stood a burned and blackened canopy bed and a partially burned dressing table with its tarnished mirror. To the left, an open door connected this room to the sitting room beyond. Maggie saw that much of the sitting room floor was gone, and sunshine poured into it from the huge holes in the roof. Her breath came in gasps.

"Did the lady in the picture live here?" Laura asked.

"Not willingly."

Maggie turned and looked at the right wall. There was another door there, this one closed. She knew it must lead to the dressing room, the one with the little window Frances had climbed out of.

"I've got to see the dressing room," she said. "You don't have to come with me."

"No, I'll stay right here and have my

phone ready to call for help when you plummet though the floor."

Maggie sidled around the perimeter of the room. After reaching the corner intact, she turned left and inched toward the door, reaching gingerly for the door knob. She almost expected it to still be hot after seventy years. The knob turned, and pushing the door open, she held her breath.

The dressing room showed smoke damage, but didn't seem to be as burned as other rooms they had seen. Maggie tested the floor in front of her and took a step. Straight ahead on the other side of the room an open door showed the bathroom beyond. To the right, a U-shaped clothes rack full of clothes filled the space. Ladies' clothes filled most of the rack, but little girls' clothes hung on one side. Maggie crept over to the side with the girls' clothes and looked through them. One of them, a light blue dress with beautiful smocking across the chest, was the dress Frances had been wearing the first time they met. She lifted it off the hanger. The fragile fabric was stained with smoke, but the dress was still recognizable. Maggie hugged it: a tangible connection to the girl in her dream.

Turning toward the tiny window that looked out over the back garden, she saw a chair in front of it, and a large wooden wardrobe on either side. She sidestepped back past the doorway and made her way to the first wardrobe, pulling the doors open.

"What on earth are you looking for?" called Laura. "I want to get out of here!"

Glamorous evening gowns filled the wardrobe. Silks and satins, fur and sequins. They were all fabulous. Maggie fought the temptation to grab an armful of the vintage gowns and take them home. After closing the wardrobe, she moved to kneel on the chair and look out the window. Ivy covered almost every square inch, but she could see the back garden through the gaps, and the strip of forest where she had hidden to wait for Frances.

With a sigh, she turned to the other wardrobe. The doors seemed to be stuck. She gave the handle a vigorous pull, and the whole room creaked and shifted. Laura shrieked, and Maggie bit her tongue to keep from doing the same. Bracing her hand on the left side of the wardrobe, she pulled again with her right. The door sprung open. Maggie opened the left side too and looked inside. Elegant silky nightgowns and dressing gowns hung on the rod. Thinking she saw something in the back right corner, she cautiously pulled the garments aside.

A sound somewhere between a sigh and a groan escaped her.

"What is it?" Laura yelled.

"I found them," she said. Two skeletons crouched in the corner, one with its arms wrapped protectively around the other. They must have died of smoke inhalation. Maggie stood and stared. She didn't feel fear or horror. Instead, hot tears rolled down her cheeks and her chest heaved with sobs. That sweet little girl! She covered the bodies again and closed the wardrobe doors.

Still holding the photo and the dress, she picked her way back to Laura. "They're both dead," she said. Laura's eyes almost popped out of her head.

"Who? Who's dead?"

"Bess and Frances."

They picked their way back to the stairs and down to the kitchen. Still weeping, Maggie stopped dead in her tracks when she saw someone waiting outside by Laura's car.

"May I ask why you two ladies have disturbed the peace of Moorhouse?"

An elderly lady gazed at them with piercing black eyes.

Maggie swallowed, trying to quell her weeping. She had been caught red-handed. She still held the picture and the dress.

"I was looking for proof that Bess and Frances Mayhew had been held prisoner here, and I found it," she said.

The older woman's face changed the instant she heard the names.

"Aye, they were held here all right, poor things," she said. "My mother was the housekeeper here, you see. Young Frances was about my age. I tried to befriend her, but every time I was caught talking to her I was punished."

"Why didn't someone let them out during the fire? I found their bodies up there, in the wardrobe."

The old lady sighed. "You found them? Oh, what a shame. That was a sad business, that fire. It's my belief that Lord Douglas set it himself. He tired of waiting for Mrs. Mayhew to submit to his desires."

"But I heard he was in Bermuda at the time of the fire!"

247

"Oh, no, lassie. That's what he paid the staff to say. When the fire started, he ran down the stairs telling everyone to get out. He said the Mayhews had already been taken to safety."

Tears glinted in her eyes.

"That lying bastard. He stood on the lawn with us watching the house burn, not lifting a finger to stop it, and then he drove off in his big blue car before the firemen arrived. We never saw him again. I suppose he really did go to Bermuda then."

"Why didn't you tell anyone about the Mayhews?"

"Oh, I did, love. But you must remember, I was just a wee child and all the adults contradicted me. They were that afraid of Lord Douglas, you know. I still come here of a Sunday afternoon and ask God to forgive the wickedness that went on here. I'm glad you found the truth. Do you suppose we can get a proper burial for that poor lady and little Frances?"

"I think we can arrange something. I'll ask Matthew Mayhew about it when I see him again."

The truth was, Maggie hoped she could somehow stop the fire from happening. She remained silent during the drive home, despite Laura's nonstop barrage of questions.

"Look," she said when they had reached her house and gone inside for a cup of tea, "I don't know what to tell you. It started with that cameo I found. It belonged to Bess Mayhew. I had to find out what happened to her. I . . . I feel responsible for her and little Frances."

Laura shrugged. "Well, are you going to report the bodies?"

"Not yet. There's something I have to do first."

That evening, Maggie rummaged through her bathroom cabinet until she found the prescription sleep aid left over from when she had her wisdom teeth out. Once again, she built up the fire in her bedroom. This time she wore the cameo around her neck and laid the dress and the photo in her lap after she propped herself up with pillows.

"Please, God," she prayed, "let me stay long enough to help."

# Cameo

The setting sun sank behind the black bulk of Moorhouse. For the first time, Frances did not appear as soon as Maggie did. Maggie shivered a little as she got into place behind some shrubs that bordered the kitchen garden. She watched the ivy as the dusk deepened into twilight and then night. Now she couldn't see a thing except the lights in the kitchen windows and a few others. The lights in the Mayhews' quarters were on also.

After what seemed like forever, the lights in the upstairs bedroom went out. A few minutes later, a dim light appeared in the little dressing room window. Maggie glimpsed the silhouette of a head and shoulders before the light went out. She stood up, every sense on alert. Then she heard the pattering of little feet on the grass.

"Frances!" she whispered.

The footsteps stopped. Maggie whispered again. "It's me, Maggie."

A faint whisper came back. "The nice lady who wants to help me?"

"Yes."

A moment later she wrapped her arms

around Frances' lithe little body. The girl had the sense to wear a warm cardigan over her thin cotton dress.

As the two of them walked hand in hand along a path through the woods, the moon rose golden and enormous, as if eager to light their errand. Maggie picked up the pace.

"Are you sure you know the way to your grandparents' house?" she asked.

Frances gave an exasperated sigh. "Everybody knows where my granny and grandfather live."

They walked on in silence for over an hour. The rising moon illuminated the lane where they walked and made the stone fences gleam like silver.

"Are we getting close?" Maggie asked. She was almost dragging Frances along now. Probably the only exercise the kid got was climbing up and down the ivy.

"There it is!" Frances pointed.

They were on a rise and Maggie saw a tiny village nestled in a depression some half a mile away. Much closer a large mansion gleamed in the moonlight, one with a much friendlier profile than Moorhouse, at least in Maggie's prejudiced opinion. Now it was Frances who ran and pulled Maggie along.

"That's Uncle Matthew's room," she said, pointing to a pair of dimly lit windows on the second floor. "He's probably still up studying because he's sitting his O Levels in a few weeks."

She giggled. "Let's surprise him."

After retrieving a key from under a flower pot, she led the way through the servants' entrance and up a back staircase to a door on the second floor. Grinning at Maggie, she knocked loudly.

"I'm just going to bed, Mother," came a male voice.

"I'm not your mother," Frances said in her clear, little-girl voice.

A crash sounded within, and then the door was thrown open by a rather scrawny teenaged boy with dark hair that sprouted from his head like a fountain.

"Franny!" he said, scooping her into his arms. "My little snapdragon, my apple blossom! Where on earth have you been all these months?"

Then he lifted his eyes and saw Maggie. His jaw dropped, and he lowered Frances back on to her feet.

"And who's your very attractive lady friend?"

Maggie offered her hand in greeting. "My name is Maggie and we need your help and we may have very little time."

He waved them into his study and listened as they told him an abbreviated version of the w hole story.

"So you see," said Maggie, "we need you to help us rescue Bess right now, tonight."

Matthew looked at Frances, whose bruises were only too evident in the light of his study lamp.

"I can't take on Duncan by myself," he said.

"You don't have to," Maggie said. "I think I've got it sorted out. Is there someone else you can call on to help?"

"MacGregor!" Matthew yelled.

A trim, impeccably dressed man in his forties appeared as if by magic.

"This is my valet, MacGregor. He was a hero in the last war, and he's still better than any two other men. He'll help if I ask him to."

"All right," said Maggie. "I assume you can drive, Mr. MacGregor?"

"Yes, ma'am."

"Well, you two must drive over to Moorhouse—as close as you can get without being heard. Then climb up the ivy to the dressing room window. It'll be a tight squeeze, but I think you can both make it. Get Bess to hide in the dressing room while you stand guard in the bedroom.

"Frances and I will stay here and give you, say, half an hour before we call the police. When the police drive up to Moorhouse, Duncan will try to hide or hurt Bess, and that's what you've got to prevent, right? So barricade the door and have some weapons handy if he manages to get in before the police do."

"And then," said Matthew, "if it all ends well, we return triumphant and you agree to marry me, right?"

Maggie laughed. "You're too young for me now, Matthew, and the next time I see you, you'll be too old."

"I am not too young!" he said. "How old are you anyway?"

"Twenty-five. And don't you know it's rude to ask? Now get going."

"Can't I come too, Uncle Matthew?"

Frances gave him a pleading look.

He knelt down and looked her in the eye.

"Now look here, my little mango tree,"

he said, "I'm counting on you to send the police to rescue your mother and me and MacGregor. Remember, according to your heartless friend here, she could disappear at any moment."

Frances hugged him. "Don't let Duncan hurt mother," she said.

"If Duncan lays a finger on her he'll wish he'd never been born. And that's on top of what he'll get for touching you."

Maggie hugged Frances and moments later watched as the car rolled quietly out to the road and turned toward Moorhouse. She looked at the grandfather clock. 1:47.

"Frances," she said, "when the clock says fifteen past two, we've got to wake up your grandfather and get him to call the police. I think it will be taken more seriously if he makes the call."

She sat on the settee and Frances climbed into her lap. One by one, they watched the minutes tick by.

"Why do you think you found me in your sleep?" asked Frances.

"It's the cameo," said Maggie. "I found the cameo with your picture on it, and then bang! Every time I fell asleep I found myself with you."

The little girl's eyes lit up.

# Cameo

"It worked! Mother prayed and prayed for a way to let people know where she was. Then she got the idea of having me drop the cameo outside near the back drive of Moorhouse. She hoped someone would find it and wonder who it belonged to and why it was there—and that it would lead them to Duncan. There have been ever so many ladies who have come here like you, you know, but none of them would help us no matter how much I asked."

"Well, I suppose it's a good thing I eventually found it," Maggie said.

The clock chimed once for the quarter hour. Frances leapt up. "I'm going to get Grandfather."

Maggie followed her down the hallway to another door, and Frances pounded on it with her little fist.

Maggie awoke in a room flooded with sunshine. Her gaze flew to the clock on her bed stand. She was already late for work. She kicked her legs in frustration. Not now!

The minute she got off work, she called Laura.

"Laura," she said, "I need to go back

out to Moorhouse. Can you please take me out there?"

"What, now?"

"Yes, now. I don't know how it turned out. I don't know if the grandfather called the police. I have to know, Laura."

"Well, I'm not going out there again. You can borrow my car, but I'm not going with you. It's creepy. And there are dead people there."

Half an hour later Maggie was on her way to Moorhouse in Laura's car. She had been able to think of nothing else all day. She got quite a shock when she turned off the road and on to the drive that led to Moorhouse. The drive was paved and well-kept. The flower-filled meadow held a couple of cows that gave her thoughtful looks as she drove past. Then she looked ahead to the house and stomped on the brakes so hard her head hit the steering wheel.

The house had vanished. There was no sign of Moorhouse as she'd seen it only yesterday. In its stead she saw a much smaller, much more modern-looking house made of grey stone, and surrounded by colorful informal gardens. Maggie sat there for a few minutes, trying to take it in. Well, she had to know. She drove forward again, and pulled up in front of the attractive stone house.

After getting out of the car, she walked to the front door on shaking legs. She clutched the cameo in her hand, not sure why she had brought it.

The door was opened by a very tall, very handsome young man with sandy hair and laughing green eyes.

"Maggie!" he said. "So you've come at last!"

He shook her hand vigorously, his large mouth grinning from ear to ear. She had never seen this man in her life. Who on earth could he be? And how did he know her name?

"Granny!" he called. "It's Maggie! She's come at last!"

"I'm Gerald, by the way," he said, as he ushered her into a comfortable sitting room. "Granny will be here in a moment." Maggie heard the tap and shuffle of approaching feet and then a spry old lady came into the room. She had snow-white hair and bright, china-blue eyes. She held out her hands to Maggie.

"Maggie! How lovely you look. Just like I remember you. I've been waiting ever so long to thank you, my dear."

Maggie gaped at her.

"It's me, Frances," said the old lady. "You helped me escape from Moorhouse and rescue my mother."

"Then your grandfather made the call and the police went to Moorhouse?"

"Yes, yes, thanks to you. When Duncan realized he was well and truly trapped, he shot himself, thus saving the government the expense of a trial. Uncle Matthew and MacGregor were the heroes of the day and we all agreed it would be too hard to try and explain your involvement, so we didn't."

"But what happened to Moorhouse?"

"Oh, you see, I knew you would come back here someday. Looking for me, of course. So Uncle Matthew and I talked my grandfather into buying the place for my mother and of course she had that hateful house torn down as soon as the war ended and she had remarried. She built this house in its place—a house of joy instead of sorrow. Gerald here is my grandson. He's been staying with me while working on his dissertation, and I've told him all about you and how pretty and resourceful you are."

Maggie's cheeks grew hot and she found herself unable to look at Gerald.

"Uh, Frances," she said, "I've brought you something. It's yours, anyway."

She pulled out the cameo and placed it in Frances' hand. The old lady gasped.

"Mother's cameo! You've kept it safe all these years."

Maggie laughed. "No, I've only kept it safe for two days," she said. "And I can't tell you how glad I am to be able to give it back to you!"

Frances put the chain around her neck and fastened it before giving Maggie a warm hug.

Maggie clung to the old lady, her eyes filled with tears of relief and gratitude. Frances was alive and happy after all these years! A weight had been lifted.

"You simply must stay for supper," said Gerald. "I make a killer beef curry and I could use some help in the kitchen."

That night when Maggie went to sleep, she didn't dream about Frances at all. Gerald, however, had a starring role.

## End

**Linda Burklin** has been a storyteller and writer since childhood. Raised primarily in Africa, she wrote for and edited her college newspaper for two years while earning her English degree. For seventeen years, she has taught writing classes to her own and other homeschooled children, and authored the *Story Quest* creative writing curriculum. She has written a memoir, several short stories, and five novels. Her passion is speculative fiction.

**Clay's Fire**
By Kat Heckenbach

Clay appeared in the bedroom doorway clutching a stack of papers, a wide grin set across his face.

"Turn off the TV, Katie. I just finished my latest story. I want to read it to you."

I reached over the pillow and grabbed the remote from the nightstand. The flickering glow from the television snapped off, leaving the room in almost complete darkness. Clay walked over and turned on the small lamp clipped to the edge of the desk against the far wall.

"Is this the one you were working on the other day? When you wouldn't let me in the study?"

"Yeah, that's it. Now settle in. Close your eyes." The chair creaked with the all-too familiar sound of him leaning back.

"Just this once can't you sit by me?"

"Katie, come on. I can't read with you watching me."

"I'll keep my eyes closed, I promise."

Clay laughed. "You'll keep them closed anyway." The chair creaked again. "Now be quiet."

I pulled the sheets up to my shoulders

and rested my head against the pillow. The last thing I saw before closing my eyes was the silhouette of the footboard that served as a wall between us.

"Ready?" Clay said, his voice already deepening into the storyteller mode I fell in love with.

"Yes."

Clay's voice drifted through the room, deep and resonating. Smooth. His words caressed me, soothing me, even when he read something terrifying. I never felt safer than when he spoke in that mystical, storyteller voice...

Charles entered the convenience store at exactly seven-thirty. The clang of the bell ended abruptly when the door slammed shut behind him. The store was crowded, and Charles felt heat climb up his neck.

Too many people in this small space, with its narrow aisles stuffed full of junk. Bags and boxes of chemical-laden snacks in their neat little rows along the shelves.

I knew that part of the story came from Clay's own fear of small spaces. Claustrophobia to the nth degree in his case. Our house had gobs of windows and soaring high ceilings. I felt a pang of discomfort, knowing Clay had mentally put himself in Charles' shoes and experienced the heat and fear of the crowded and confined store, the kind of place he'd never willingly enter in real life.

People milled around Charles, avoiding each other's eyes, as if stopping in to buy a six-pack and a bag of Fritos were some sort of conspiratorial act. He lowered his eyes as well, tugging at the collar of his shirt.

Tight...so tight.

I pulled at the sheets. Hadn't they only been up to my shoulders? Why were they pushing against my chin?

Charles' neck was slick with perspiration, and as he stood in front of the newspaper rack, beads of sweat popped up on his forehead. He swiped his hands through his bangs, the heat from his forehead surging into his palms.

"I must have a fever," he whispered to himself.

The sheets suddenly smothered me, sticking to my legs. I folded the edge over and kicked myself free, trying to stay tuned in to Clay's voice. Air, not quite cool enough, hit my skin and I settled back into my pillow.

Charles began searching for the shelf that held aspirin, sweat pouring into his eyes. He glanced sideways. No one seemed to notice him. Heat flooded him, and he swallowed. His tongue felt as if it would crack from the effort.

Maybe the aspirin would have to come later. Right now, a drink. He took a swaying step toward the soda fountain. His hand groped the collar of his shirt again. It was soaked, but grated his skin like sandpaper. He peeled off his jacket and dropped it on the floor. Two more stumbling steps and he stood in front of the soda fountain. He dared a look around. A few people threw him tentative glances, but their eyes immediately diverted.

I licked my lips and slid up against my pillow so I could reach for the glass of water on the nightstand. My arm slid across the pillowcase, now slimy from the sweat that had soaked through my hair. Had Clay turned the heater on just to make his story feel more real? I listened hard as I swallowed the last gulps of water in the glass. His voice seemed deeper than usual, even more melodic, like the bass guitar in a haunting ballad.

The paper cup trembled in Charles's

hand. Ice tumbled out as he pressed the cup against the lever. Each cube that touched his hand burned in opposition to his hot skin and melted almost immediately.

"This isn't right," he said out loud, not caring now who looked at him.

He slammed the cup into the next lever and soda poured out, sloshing over the sides and sizzling as it hit his skin. He drew the cup to his mouth with both shaking hands, spilling the sticky liquid down his sweat-encrusted shirt.

He gulped, and the drink only turned to steam in his mouth, scalding his lips and the insides of his nostrils as he inhaled. He dumped the remains over his head, listening to the sputter of liquid popping into gas around his head.

The glass had slipped out of my hand and hit the floor with a clang, but Clay continued to read. His voice wrapped around me and the intensity of it prickled my skin from head to toe. I reached into my tingling hair and felt that the sweat had dried completely…

Bodies shifted around Charles, and his breath caught in his throat as he gazed around at their staring faces. His neck muscles squeezed and released, allowing the scalding air to finally escape his lungs. A woman backed away, a look of horror contorting her face. Her scream threatened to shatter his bones, which pulsed heat along with his heartbeat.

My pulse thrummed in my ear, nearly drowning out Clay's voice. I scrambled to find his words again, even while my mind screamed for me to turn away from him. I needed him to soothe me through the story. But the harder I focused on his voice, the more the heat flamed.

Charles heaved in breath after breath, as flames licked the inside of his body, searing tissue and bone.

"Help me!" he cried to the crowd as they finally began to back away. The terror in the eyes of some scared him less than the look of morbid curiosity in others.

Questions swirled around his mind— What's happening? Why aren't they doing something? Am I dying?

The expressions on their faces as they clawed past each other said, "Yes, yes you are…."

(Clay, am I dying…?)

Charles tore at his clothing, and it crumbled in his hand. Blackened with ash from the flames that had finally pushed through to the surface of his skin.

Flames...fire...coming from inside him...

The heat reached beyond anything Charles had imagined.

(I see the flames, Clay! Please stop! I see them...)

And just as the phrase entered his mind..."spontaneous combustion"...the heat seared even higher and with a burst—

Air poured into my lungs as I gasped. The sudden absence of Clay's voice resonated in my ears...silence smothering me as I sprang from the bed. I'd felt the heat so intensely I'd imagined seeing flames—a sudden burst of light just as Clay stopped reading.

The dim light from the desk lamp glowed around the edge of the footboard, but the rest of the room lay heavy with darkness.

"Clay, what happened?"

No response.

My hands began to tremble, and I threw my legs over the side of the bed. My nightgown clung to me, and as I ran my fingers through my bangs I found my hair sticky with sweat as well.

I forced myself to stand, and stepped around the corner of the bed. The desk lamp cast its dim light on the pile of ashes in the flame-scorched desk chair that still leaned back.

## End

**Kat Heckenbach grew up in a small town, where she spent** most of her time either drawing or sitting in her "reading tree" with her nose buried in a fantasy novel...except for the hours pretending her back yard was an enchanted forest that could only be reached through the secret passage in her closet. She never could give up on the idea that maybe she really was magic, mistakenly placed in a world not her own—but as the years passed, and no elves or fairies carted her away, she realized she was just going to have to create the life of her fantasies with words. Her characters always find a secret world—whether it be real, imaginary, or in the pages of a book. Enter Kat's not-so-secret world at www.katheckenbach.com.

**Ghost Roommate**
By Matthew Sketchley

It had been a long day, and all I really wanted was to come home, get something to eat, and fall asleep on the couch watching Family Feud. But even as I turned the handle to my apartment door, I knew that wasn't going to happen.

"Nick," a voice floated through the air from my living room. "Niiick..."

I closed my eyes and, for just a second, considered turning around and finding a hotel. But I'd have to come back here sooner or later anyway, seeing as I lived here. And so did Larry. Well, not really. See, Larry was my roommate, but not the normal kind.

Before I could sum up the willpower to open the door, Larry's head stuck out from the middle. "Nick!" He shouted. "You're late. Come on, get in here, I'm starving."

I shook my head and pushed the door open through him. "You shouldn't be able to eat, you're a ghost. It should just fall through you." I pushed past him, or tried to—with ghosts, you end up just walking through them—into my apartment.

270

"Nu-uh," Larry whined, following me down the hall. "I can eat."

"Then why is it that whenever it's your turn to clean the apartment your hands always go right through the vacuum cleaner?"

I didn't bother to look over my shoulder, but I knew he was making the same hurt expression he always did. "I don't know, I guess metal interferes with it. Lay off, I feel bad enough about it already."

"The vacuum's plastic, Larry." Not that it really mattered. He was always going to find some way to weasel out of doing his share of the chores, and I'd learned to deal with that long ago.

I went into the kitchen, ignoring his protests, and opened up the fridge. The only thing in there was a pizza box.

I spun around to glare at Larry, but I couldn't see him. "Don't turn invisible," I snapped, "I know you're still there."

A haze appeared just to my left, and it resolved into Larry, wearing a sheepish grin. "Told you I could eat."

I took a deep breath. Yelling at Larry would just make the neighbors think I was even crazier. "You ate everything in the

# Ghost Roommate

fridge," I said slowly, "and then you ordered a pizza?"

Larry shrugged. "You could afford it. It's all good, I left you a slice." He pointed at the box.

I reached into the fridge and grabbed the box, pulling it out and hearing a lone piece of pizza slide around inside. I brandished it at him. "Seriously? You got it from Mike's? You know that place is disgusting, right?"

Larry pointed at his mouth. "Dead. No sense of taste."

"Then why did you—you know what, never mind. Can't you just go haunt someone else?"

"I told you, I saw a cockroach in the kitchen so I was too afraid to eat and I starved to death and now I'm stuck here." He told me a different story about dying each time, but maybe this one was true. Maybe that was why he was always eating now. The worst kind of ghost was a hungry ghost.

I leaned back against the counter. Why did Larry always have to be so exhausting? "Yeah, sure, but couldn't you haunt one of the other apartments? Sylvia next door probably deserves it."

Larry's eyes widened. "No way man, she scares me."

He did have a point. I went back into the living room and plopped myself down on the couch, taking the cold slice of pizza out of the box. At least he hadn't gotten anything weird on this one. I flipped on the TV and chewed at the pizza in silence, wondering what to do about Larry. I had to admit that when he wasn't being annoying the company could be nice, but he had no concept of personal space. As evidenced by the fact that he decided to sit so close to me that my right arm was actually inside him.

"You know," I said after a moment, "the first time you showed up here I thought I'd just had some bad ravioli."

Larry turned his head away from the screen to look at me. "That's why you should never eat pasta from a can, Nick. Like I always say."

I shook my head a bit, but I was too tired to do more than that. "You've never said that."

"Well, I'm going to start saying it now. People need to know about this kind of thing."

In spite of myself, I gave a slight

laugh. I was still mad at him, but all of a sudden I was just too exhausted to care. "Seriously though, what's it going to take for you to give me some space?"

"Your soul, probably."

I grunted. It wasn't the first time he'd joked about wanting my soul, but I wished he'd stop. There was something about the idea that just creeped me out, and the fact that he was a ghost made me wonder if it was actually possible. It sounded ridiculous, but I hadn't believed in ghosts either until I moved here and met this weirdo. That being said, sometimes I might consider it if it would get him out of my hair.

After a few minutes of silently watching the commercials, the game show came back on. I dropped the empty pizza box on the coffee table, wishing there was more food. I'd have to hop out to the store in the morning, but I was too tired tonight. And I wouldn't trust Larry to do the shopping even if he could.

"Hey," Larry said, interrupting the TV. "Does this count as cuddling?"

I sighed. Why did he always wait until the commercials were over to say something stupid? "No, we're just taking up the same space, because you don't understand how boundaries work."

Larry shifted in his seat a bit, but didn't move away from me. "Oh. That's too bad, since paranormal romance is huge right now. It'd be great for ratings."

I didn't even bother to glance over at him. "Do you think we're on a reality show?"

"No, but I'm saying if we were, that'd be good for ratings."

"Larry?"

"Yeah?"

"You're an idiot."

He gave me a playful shove. "It'd be a great show. I'd watch us."

I waved my hand at the air. "You know what? This is crazy, I'm going to find an exorcist or something."

"Hey, hey, hey," Larry floated up in front of me. "You don't need to do that. If you've got a problem let's talk, don't just threaten to kick me out."

I shook my head. "No. No, you're not making me look like the bad guy here. You're always getting in the way, you ate all my food, not for the first time, and you're dead. I'm pretty sure you're not supposed to be hanging around here."

# Ghost Roommate

"You're not really going to blame me for being dead, are you? I think I've suffered enough." Larry looked like he was actually taking this seriously. Finally.

There had to be some way we could compromise on this. "Look," I said, "do you know why you're stuck here? Was there something you never got to do, did they not find your body, what's the problem?"

Larry frowned, obviously really uncomfortable. "I was skipping rope on the balcony and fell down. No big deal."

"We don't have a balcony, Larry, I'm paying five hundred dollars a month for this place. We barely have a fire escape."

"Look, just forget about it, okay?" Larry demanded. "I don't want to talk about it right now."

"Fine, fine, no exorcists." I let the subject drop. But I didn't forget it.

The next day, I spent my lunch break at the library doing some research. It wasn't that I didn't like Larry, but having him around so much kind of grated on the nerves. Plus, part of me felt bad for the guy, trapped in a dingy apartment. Whatever the real story was, I didn't think it was a very happy one. He might not want to tell me why he was haunting my place, but maybe I could at least figure out what had turned him into a ghost. Once I got that, maybe I could figure out how to free him. He couldn't really want to just hang around forever, could he?

The librarian gave me a weird look when I asked for the paranormal section, but I was used to that from the few times I'd tried to explain Larry to my friends. I found the books pretty easily, and packed up eight or nine before heading back to work. One was a do-it-yourself exorcism guide, just in case nothing else helped. Deep down, I believed Larry wanted to move on. I know I wanted him to.

I don't remember if I got much done at work that afternoon. The whole time passed by in a blur, sneaking the occasional bathroom break to skim through a chapter. I think it was a slow day, so nobody really cared. It was when I read chapter two of *Ghosts and Demons: A Comparative Study,* a book I'd picked up just on impulse, that I realized I had to be careful.

*"Some ghosts may resist eviction from the*

*mortal plane, if they feel it will hurt whatever mission has kept them behind, or if they simply fear death. While they may or may not otherwise desire to inflict harm, a ghost in such a desperate state can exhibit behavioral patterns similar to that of a more malevolent entity, such as an imp or even a demon."*

I had never imagined Larry as dangerous, but he did keep changing the subject if I brought his death and he never would tell me the real story. Maybe he was just joking around, or maybe he was afraid, but I knew sending him on would be the best choice. A tiny one-bedroom apartment was no place to live forever. Or, well... exist forever. He wasn't really living, per se. But, he might try to stop me. I decided to hide the books from him. Turns out, that was the best decision I could have made.

It was a clear day, so I went to the park after work to read, where Larry couldn't bother me. That worked for the moment, but I knew that when I got home, I'd have to find a place to hide them from him. The laundry hamper would probably work. He never did go near anything that reminded him of chores. *Maybe he died in a dish washing accident,* I thought.

Resolving to protect my books behind a fortress of unwashed clothing, I packed up and headed back to the apartment. On the way, I tried to think of how exactly I would stop Larry from looking into my bag if he decided to get curious, but I figured I'd just wing it. I tried to tell myself he probably wouldn't even want to randomly stare inside my bag, but that kind of logic only applied to sane people, and I was dealing with Larry.

Sure enough, as soon as I walked into the apartment, he stuck his head out from the ceiling to greet me. "Hey, Nick, you're late. Did you go shopping after work? What did you get me?" He didn't stick his face into my bag, but he definitely stared at it for way too long.

I shook my head. "I didn't get you anything, I just decided to take a walk in the park. It's the first nice day of the year, I didn't want to just spend it inside."

Larry gestured around. "I spent it inside. It was pretty chill."

I glared at him. "You didn't clean out the fridge again, did you? I just bought a week's worth of food this morning." I'd gotten up early to do it, too. Being hungry had helped.

# Ghost Roommate

"No, I wouldn't do that twice in a row. And you only bought three days' worth," he added. "You know I need a steady diet or I'll waste away to nothing."

"You already did," I muttered, stepping inside and closing the door. "You're dead, remember?" As I walked down the hall, I wondered for a second if that might have been insensitive. I was never really sure how dead people felt about having it pointed out to them. Larry was the only one I'd met.

He didn't seem to mind. "Oh yeah, forgot. So when are you going to give me that stuff you bought?" Honestly, I was a little surprised he hadn't already started rifling through my bag. All that work on teaching him about boundaries must have finally been paying off.

"I didn't buy you anything," I reminded him. "I didn't buy anything at all, I just went for a walk." It was true, mostly.

I went into my bedroom, ignoring his jabbering, and looked at my closet. Perfect, I'd left it open this morning. Now I just had to toss my bag in oh-so-casually, and call on my old high school basketball training...

The bag landed square in my laundry

hamper.

Larry floated through me from behind —I saw my life flash before my eyes whenever he did that—and peered into the closet. "Nice shot!" It didn't sound like he suspected anything.

I grinned. "I guess I've still got it." Why would he suspect anything, anyway? He wasn't exactly the brightest guy in the world.

Larry tried to high-five me, but his hand went through mine and it threw him off balance. "So," he said when he steadied himself, "what's the plan for tonight?"

I shrugged. "I don't know, not too much. I'm working early tomorrow, so I probably shouldn't stay up too late."

Larry punched me on the arm. This time he remembered to actually make contact, however it was he did that. "Want to go out on the town?"

"I just told you I was going to bed early." I narrowed my eyes. "And you can't leave the apartment."

"It's true. Not since I tried running with scissors."

Did he think it was funny now? His feelings about death never seemed to stay the same. Come to think of it, his feelings on anything seemed to change every few minutes. I'd never thought about it before, but Larry was pretty unstable.

"I think I'll just watch a movie," I told him, trying to sound natural. I was absolutely not feeling bad for Larry, not when he was standing there annoying me. Okay, but I wasn't going to let him know I was.

Eventually, Larry and I decided on some action movie, and I spent the whole time thinking about those books I'd taken out. Even when I went to bed early, I kept looking over at my closet. Reading them would have been nice, but there was too much risk of Larry floating through on his way to the bathroom. Whatever exactly he did in there.

I went on like this for about a week, spending as much time out of the apartment as I was willing to let Larry go unchecked, and reading up on ghosts. I found all kinds of ways to defend yourself, or to prove that there was a ghost around, but no way of finding out why a ghost was there or how to properly send them away. Finally, just when I thought I was learning something useful, Larry found the books.

After a week or so, I had finally missed the hamper. That's when the dream started.

I was running through a dark hallway, but I didn't know where I was going. I felt like I was late for something. The hallway kept stretching on, until I finally saw a door to my right. I opened it up and saw that I was back in high school, and everyone was already writing the exam. I turned to apologize to the teacher, and saw that it was Larry sitting on the other side of the desk.

He grinned. "You made it! Kind of a lame dream though, I expected better. I mean come on, you're not even naked."

For a second, I wasn't sure if this really was a dream or not. Was I dreaming about Larry, or was he actually inside my dream? Could ghosts do that? "Larry, what are you doing here?"

"Well I'll tell you what I'm not doing," Larry said. "I'm not leaving, Nick."

My mouth dried out. "Oh. You, uh, you noticed those books, huh? It's not what it looks like man, I—"

Larry floated up in front of me,

cutting me off. "I'm not stupid, Nick." Something seemed different about him now. Larry smiled coldly. "So you going to give me your soul or not?"

I swallowed. "Come on man, that's not funny."

Larry's eyes glinted. "I'm done being funny. I figured I'd annoy you into submission, but I guess you're a little too resourceful for that. I've been going after your soul for a while now."

I suppressed a shiver. "Why me? Why do you want anyone's soul, anyway?"

He shrugged. "You, because I really can't leave that apartment. And you really shouldn't eat pasta from a can," he added with an ominous glare. "I don't think I really need to tell you why. But if you're not going to give it to me, I guess I'm just going to have to take it."

I took a step back. "Is that something you can do?"

"I'm not sure. Probably, yeah."

I frowned. "I'm pretty sure you're wrong about that."

"Well watch me do it, then!"

"Larry, none of the books I've read say anything about you being able to just steal a soul." I was starting to get a little less scared. "You know, it's really hard to be intimidated by you when I know more about spirits than you do. And come to think of it, it's even harder to be scared of a guy named Larry."

Larry shifted in what looked like discomfort. "Well, Nick, that's my name, so I don't know what you expect me to do about it."

"Is it short for something?" I asked. "A full name might sound a little stronger."

"Larrance."

"What?"

"It's short for Larrance."

"Laurence?"

"Larrance. Like larynx."

"What kind of name is Larrance?"

"The kind where you go by Larry. But that's beside the point," he added, switching back to that menacing tone. "Your soul. I want it!"

Crap. I'd been hoping I could keep him distracted until I woke up. "Sorry, it's not really for sale. How were you planning on getting it, anyway? Now that you know you can't just reach in and grab it, I mean."

Larry had that look he got when he was trying to come up with a story off the top of his head. "Yeah. I figured we would have some kind of contest. I saw it in a movie once. I win, I get your soul. You win, I let you wake up."

I blinked. "Wait, you can stop me from waking up?"

"Yeah, I'm a spirit. We hijack people's dreams all the time. If you ever have one of those nightmares where you're trying to wake up and you just can't? That's one of us messing with you."

Well that was new. And now I had to find a way to get out of it. "So you're just going to keep me here forever?"

"Yeah, Nick, I'm just going to keep you here. It's not that confusing."

"But what about food?" I asked. "And water? I need to be awake to get those, and I need them to live."

It was Larry's turn to blink. "Really. Did not think that one through."

I gave him a look. "Have you ever done this before?"

His face turned back into a sick grin. "No, I've only been doing this a week before you moved in. But I can feed you while you sleep. You'll be just fine." Well, that plan was down the tubes.

Suddenly, the classroom we were in dropped away and all that was left was an oppressive blackness. I could hear things moving nearby, clacking and sliding and hissing. One of the... *things*... out there came close, and I could almost see the outline of what looked like a tentacle, but it seemed to have eyes glistening and staring at me. I felt pressure growing inside of my brain, until it seemed ready to burst. Larry stood there watching me, not saying a word. He didn't seem all that bothered by the horror show that was presumably going on just outside of our vision. Then again, he was probably making it all up. Finally, he opened his mouth. "This is your new home, Nick. Let me know when you're done with that soul of yours."

And he was gone. Leaving me alone in the dark. I tried not to listen to the things moving around me, but I couldn't help but wonder if they knew I was there. I could only hope I never found out as I let the grinding and slipping noises wash over me.

It all stretched into what seemed an eternity, and before long I was almost certain that the only reason nothing had come any closer was that whatever was in the darkness didn't care one way or the other about me. Which made it worse in a way. At first I would feel one of the...

things coming close, and I would shy away, hoping it never developed the curiosity to take a look at me.

Then, after a while, I started waiting for them to come near. Even though I didn't know if I would ever be able to see them, I wondered if they were looking at me. I had a loneliness like I'd never experienced before, and I began to wonder how I could get these horrors to come a little closer, maybe show some interest in me.

After a few months I figured they must be bored, so I decided to tell them a story. I had to think for a bit, but eventually I decided the only story really worth telling was about Larry.

So, that's how I got here. Was that interesting enough?

Are you still there?

End

**Matthew Sketchley** is currently a student at Carleton University in Ottawa, Ontario. He writes whenever possible and has involved himself with student theater by writing, directing, acting, and even working backstage in various productions. In this atmosphere he gained a love for short, strange comedy, which shows through in his stories.

**Baby, don't cry**
By R V Saunders

"Give me back that Honshu Baby."

"No. Shan't."

Geraldine held the doll high above her head, it's legs and arms hanging limply from its body.

"Give it back, or I shall call your Mum."

Indecision whirred through Geraldine's mind, as she weighed up the strength of the threat.

"You wouldn't."

"Would, too."

Geraldine smiled. "She won't be able to hear you, she's playing her music downstairs. She never hears anything when she's playing her music."

Emma strained to hear. Yes, there it was, the rhythmic thump, thump coming up through the floor. She'd tried calling to Geraldine's mum before, but it hadn't worked, not when the music was on downstairs. Her voice just wasn't strong enough.

Geraldine's grin grew wider. "If you want it, you can have it. But you'll have to come and get it," and with that she strained her arm up even higher, so that the doll's nose almost touched the mobile that swung gently from the lampshade.

# Baby, don't cry

Emma's face stayed calm, almost composed. Finally, after a few seconds of thought, she looked up and simply said, "OK." With a slow shuffle of her hips she started to lever herself off the chair, the toes of her right foot straining to touch the ground.

Geraldine looked on in fascination, her eyes fixed on her friend's left pants-leg. It hung loose, as it always did, with no leg to give it any shape. Finally, Emma eased her weight onto her one foot, and looked back up at the doll that hung tantalisingly out of reach. Then, holding onto the edge of the bed with one hand, she began to hop towards Geraldine. She stretched her free hand out in front of her towards the doll, but Geraldine edged it further away with each hop.

"How can I come and get it, if you keep moving away from me?" Emma asked. But Geraldine said nothing, and simply watched her friend make a final stretch before giving up, collapsing down onto the floor in a messy heap.

Emma continued from the floor. "But your Mum gave me that after the accident, to show that I wasn't really different. Because all of your other friends had them

... and ... and ...", but she could say no more. Her face fell flat, as if some beacon of hope had been switched off inside her.

Geraldine stared intently at her friend. Was she going to cry? Geraldine had never seen her friend cry before, not even after the accident. Geraldine knew that for sure, because she had been there when it had happened, when the car had gone over Emma's leg.

But Emma didn't cry. She just sat there, staring down at her one good leg, not saying a word.

Eventually Geraldine realised that her arm was beginning to ache, and she let it drop to her side, the doll's head lolling about as she did so. Maybe Emma would cry if she kicked her. Or pinched her. Geraldine had cried when her brother had pinched her, and couldn't think of anything in the world that hurt more, not when the pinch seemed like it would never end, it just went on and on.

Yes, she would pinch her. But where? Slowly, silently, she tiptoed around her friend, her eyes scouring the exposed flesh. Without even looking, she cast the doll to the far side of the room, her eyes never leaving Emma. She would pinch her on the inside of her arm, just above the elbow. That was where Geraldine's brother had pinched her.

Suddenly, with a jolt, her friend sat up, her back as straight as a ruler. Geraldine froze, her hand hovering above her friend, fingers out-stretched. "What is it?" she asked, glaring at Emma. Her friend squirmed around to meet her gaze.

"It's the front door. Somebody just knocked on the front door." In two steps Geraldine moved over to the window, and squashed her cheek hard against the cold glass. By craning her neck she could just see the front door and a man standing outside in a dull brown uniform, his bald head winking up at her in the sunlight. As she looked, the door opened and her Mum's dark hair bobbed into view. They must have said something, because then the man held up a small pad, which Mum signed. Then, reaching down, he picked up a brown cardboard box, and handed it to Mum, before walking away, back to his van.

Finally, once she was sure that the drama had finished, Geraldine turned back to her friend. "It was just some man giving a box to Mum." Maybe in a bit she would go down and ask Mum what was in the box. Then she smiled as she remembered what she'd been about to do. Her friend still sat there, empty pants leg taunting her.

But before Geraldine could do anything, she heard the stairs creak. It was Mum, she knew without looking. Mum always came up the stairs one at a time in slow, delicate steps. Not like Dad, who crashed his way up two or even three at a time.

And then the bedroom door opened, and Mum came in, all smiles and laughter. Geraldine stood her ground, carefully eyeing the way her Mum was hiding something behind her back. "Geraldine, I've got a present for your friend."

At that Geraldine's face lit up. "Really, Mum? Can I open it?"

Geraldine's Mum looked down at her. "No Geraldine, you can't. It's a present for Emma." Mum's voice was stern, but Geraldine could see the twinkle in her eye was still there. This was going to be a good present.

Mum walked over to where Emma sat, and crouched down. By now, Emma's face had sunk back down so that her brown hair hid her face. Slowly, as if only just realising that someone else was nearby, she looked up, smiling as she recognised the face.

Mum looked Emma in the eye. "You know how you lost your leg in that accident?"

Emma nodded.

"Well, I've bought you something that will help make you better."

Geraldine was so excited now she was fit to burst. "What is it, Mum?" she asked, not waiting for her friend. "What have you got her?"

Wordlessly, her Mum drew the cardboard box from behind her back, and opened it slowly from the bottom. Geraldine strained to see what her Mum pulled out. It was pink, she could see that, and then ...

"Oh, Mum!" Now she could see the toes, and the foot and the ankle. It was a new leg for her friend, just like the old one. She could see Emma smile, but then her head was sagging again. It dropped and it dropped until it hung limply from her shoulders.

Silence hung in the air for a moment before Mum turned to Geraldine. "The instructions say it's just a plug and play, but

I think it I'll switch her off for a while just to make sure. It looks like she needs recharging for a couple of hours, anyway." So Mum reached behind Emma's neck, flipped the off switch, and gently watched her shut down.

Geraldine whined. "But, Mum!"

"No, Geraldine," said Mum, delicately picking up Emma in one hand. "You can play with her again tomorrow." Then, casting her eyes to the far corner of room to the discarded Honshu Baby. "Why don't you play with your other friend for a while?"

### End

**R V Saunders** is an award-winning writer living and working in Birmingham, England, a couple of hundred yards from where J R R Tolkien grew up. He has had over thirty short stories and poems published. After taking several years off writing to pursue a variety of other interests, he is now embarking on a new series of fantasy and science fiction short stories.

## The Water Man
By Sherry Rossman

Midnight was the lady that woke me with a stroke and made me a cripple. My head felt pierced by the devil's sword and most of my words fell out, leaving me with no way to tell my grandson how much I loved him.

I can still hug him. I can draw a heart, though a shaky one. But I can't rightly express how raising him was the best thing I ever did.

Or that I just killed a man.

Gloria, my neighbor, dressed in purple with her white hair splayed like a dandelion, pulled my hands from Tom's neck and smiled. She put her finger to her lips and we sat back and watched the gift we were given in exchange for our voices. Tom's spirit glowed brighter than I expected. Like a candle alone in the dark, he lit up, turned his head and looked at me, then rose, soft and glinting. I was hoping the sight would lift the heavy coils from my heart, and it did for about one minute before they snapped back on, squeezing it like a curse; ringing out the word, murderer, with every beat. I clung to Tom's smile, hoping there was forgiveness in it. The devil may have meant the stroke as a curse, but the Water Man gave me this sight as a gift. No one really dies.

"Deep calls to deep."

I knew she'd say that. I don't know what it means, but they're the only four words Gloria was left with after her own brush with lady midnight.

I looked back down at Tom's body. He was a pretentious white collar; he bragged day and night about his oil investments and his rare antiques that would set his kids and grandkids up for life. He stole them, of course. Tried to steal Gloria's silver bracelet that covered the tattoo on her wrist; *Deep calls to deep*, in black script. I first saw the tattoo after her husband passed on, right before she lost the rest of her words, as if she needed to be marked with those four.

I wonder if I had tattooed a few words on my skin if I could have said them too. Devil took most of the good ones. Can't even think 'em. Have to put in substitutions. It's a good thing people can't hear my thoughts.

I let my eyes fall to my hands—these hands that were only meant for good—

# The Water Man

and clenched them into fists to stop them from trembling.

Gloria gripped the blue recliner next to her and pulled herself up. She took the red scarf hanging from the wooden coat rack and covered her bruised arms with it. When she grabbed hold of the recliner again for balance, she coughed for a good two minutes, then gave Tom's body a good kick.

I'd have kicked him too, but I figured I'd done enough. He was no gentlemen. Gentlemen watch out for ladies, not take advantage of their disabilities in order to rob the daylights out of them. I don't usually care much for ladies and gentlemen; I'm more comfortable around folks, but Gloria was special. And she's like me.

She looked at Tom's body and shrugged her shoulders. Thoughts of my grandson struck me: what if they threw me in prison? Without the ability to tell him what happened, he'd think I was no better than his deadbeat parents. I can't do that to Toby.

My breath began to come quickly. I yanked on my collar, popping off buttons to let in more air. How's an old coot like me to hide a body? Tom isn't exactly a feather pillow. After fretting over this for a few minutes, I held up a finger so Gloria'd know I'd be back, and left her apartment.

The maintenance crew usually left a flat cart in the underground garage. I took the three flights of stairs to avoid running into anyone who might see guilt in my eyes. By the time I got to the first floor I had to sit on the last step to catch my breath before stepping into the garage. Almost every space was full. Everyone but me had a newer model wagon. My wagon was twenty years old, with faded paint and bald tires. I didn't need it—Toby drove me wherever I wanted to go, but I liked to know that I could drive unsupervised like I'm a full-grown adult, dagnabit.

I found the flat cart in the corner by the bathroom. I pushed it into the elevator; my hands shook as I gripped the handle, weak from having to choke Tom. I didn't mean to kill him; I was hoping he'd pass out before he croaked.

I made it to the third floor before I ran into Mark, the building director, when the door slid open. He's a poor replacement for Sheila, the former manager who had no trouble chatting with a man without words. She had that special way about her. But Mark is all business and fake smiles. The place lost something after he took over. And besides, Gloria hates him; knows something about him that she can't communicate. I nodded at him when he greeted me, and slid my hands behind the cart handle to disguise my shakes.

"Can I help you with something, Emmet?" Mark took me in with the cart, a fleeting glint of doubt in his eyes.

I shook my head and pushed the cart out, making my way down the hall. He took one step, then called after me. "I'm guessing you need to move something heavy. Let me help you."

Damn. How do I get rid of him?

Inside my apartment, I quickly looked over my furniture. Not a stick of it had any value, except my Ginny's chair. She's the one who introduced me to the Water Man. If it hadn't been for her, I would have thought he was just another myth. But it's the only thing that would make sense to Mark. I pointed to it and felt a new crack in my heart.

"To the dumpster then?"

I shook my head and pretended to steer.

"To the garage. For Toby? I'm sure he'd love anything you gave him. Didn't bat an eye when we raised the rent a few months ago. He's a good kid."

Mark's comment spiked my already pounding heart. I hadn't realized they raised the rent. When Toby decided I should move here after my stroke, I wanted to tell him not to bother—I wasn't worth his investment. Why would I need to live in a place with fancy lounges and fountains? But I suppose when you love someone as fiercely as I loved Toby, they can't help but reflect it. So here I reside, a blue collar among the starched.

When we passed Gloria's apartment, I tipped an ear toward it, but I didn't hear a thing. Usually, when someone passed to the great Beyond, she hummed an old mountain tune her grandmother taught her. She probably didn't think Tom deserved it.

Mark hauled Ginny's recliner into the bed of my wagon, made some excuse about investigating a noise complaint and winked at me in his nervous way before he shot back upstairs. He and Tom were both nervous winkers; no good ever comes from those types. After I said my goodbyes to my honey's chair, I called the elevator back down.

I made it all the way to Gloria's door before I realized I forgot the flat cart. Exhaustion tugged my old bones to the floor. To help keep my feet steady beneath me I was going to need my cane.

What I found inside my apartment nearly shocked the spirit out of me. I quickly closed the door and wobbled inside.

Tom's body lay on the floor next to my kitchen table. I lowered myself to one of the wooden chairs and ran my hands over my head. This can't be, this just can't be. Gloria couldn't have carried him here.

I made it to her apartment in a flash; my heart pumped so hard it momentarily lifted the burden of age from my legs. But it did me no good. She was gone. I checked through her bedroom, bathroom —her closets were stuffed so full of fabric I had to close them before the contents buried me in a quilted avalanche.

"Ggggg."

I grabbed her old librarian's bell from her small bookcase in the living room and rang it until my hand couldn't grip it anymore. It fell to the floor at my feet.

This couldn't have happened. I can't let the police take me like they took Toby's parents. I didn't have anything to leave him…not a penny, not a dadgum heirloom that wouldn't fall apart within a year. I had nothing to give him except to live an honorable life.

I was only trying to protect Gloria.

I kept my eyes open for spirits as I walked down the hall—surely she was still alive. The elevator was in use—I could hear a gaggle of hens loading into it on the floor below—I knew that bunch and I didn't want to see them. One by one, I took the stairs down to the garage. This time I walked past the wagons and headed for the exit door. The only one who could help me now was the Water Man.

A warm puff of air hit me as I made my way to the edge of the valley. The city lights winked on the far side, several football fields away, leaving land in between us for thinking.

*Water Man.*

The night was still enough where I could hear the steady rush of water from the stone fountain near the front entrance. I looked into the still night sky and let the sound run over my weary soul.

# The Water Man

The little creek where I sometimes met Him was nearly dried up. When I stepped closer to look into the reflection, the Milky Way peaked at me from between the twigs and rocks jutting from beneath the shallow stream. Water Man.

My skin warmed all around. I leaned my hand against the lone tree near the creek bed and peered into the shallow pool. A single spark floated from the bottom of the pool to the surface, then disappeared. I looked closer while I wiped at my eyes. I didn't mean to kill him. I'm so sorry. Despite Tom's poor character, I thought of his family, and shame spiraled from my head down to my toes.

Suddenly a gust of wind whipped my clothes tight against my skin as if pulling me away from the creek. "N-nn-nnn."

I couldn't help it. The wind rose warm and fierce as it took my breath away. I tried to look back at the creek in the hopes of seeing the Water Man, but He continued to blow me away.

Defeated, I shuffled inside to my wagon and lowered myself to the flat cart sitting behind it. Old bones. Broken voice. A killer. Who am I to still be here?

I stood and wrapped my arms around

Ginny's chair, shoved my face in the seat and wished it would unravel and sew me into the surface right where it still smelled of her lilac perfume.

When I finally pulled away, my sleeve caught on something in the seam. I tugged at it until a small silver bracelet dropped to the floor. I picked it up, turned it over where four words had been engraved in plain script: *Deep calls to deep.* Like a chilled whisper rushing through my body, I remembered that Gloria wore this when I left her with Tom's body.

Mark.

I stumbled outside to the creek where the night was still once again. With the bracelet in my hand, I held it out. I could feel my quickened heartbeat in the ends of my fingertips as I offered my burden to the Water Man.

*Deep calls to Deep.*

The words resonated within me like a bell from the center of the earth. These weren't Gloria's words—they were those of the Water Man. I had to figure out what they meant.

The front lobby was empty of all except the college student who worked the night desk. His black hair stood at attention; a stark contrast to his deep slouch over his cell phone. He jumped when I thrust the bracelet between his eyes and phone.

"Oh, Hi Emmet. Did you find this or something?"

I flipped it over and pointed at the script, then pointed at his phone. The kid took the bracelet in his hand and held it underneath his desk lamp. "Huh, this must be Gloria's."

I pointed at his phone again, two, three times, before it dawned on him.

"Oh, you want me to google it. Sure thing, man."

He punched in the phrase. "It's a poem. 'Deep calls to deep in the roar of your waterfalls; all your waves and breakers have swept over me.' Doesn't say who wrote it. Wonder what it means?" The kid's eyes widen. "Hey, if you're looking for her, she was walking out front about ten minutes ago." He held out the bracelet and pointed outside the front entrance.

I took it and gave him a nod. When I rushed outside, I paced around the building looking for Gloria. In the roar of your waterfalls...dang it. I'm no good at poetry. Ginny would have known what it meant.

Ahead of me, I thought I saw Gloria in her red scarf walking around the corner, but something wasn't right in the space to the left of her. A dark shape followed her, blocking out all light it passed over. "Gggggg…"

I clenched my hand into a fist, angry at my incompetence, then stretched it out to where it made contact with the wall. I let my hand slide along the exterior of the apartment building and jogged toward Gloria. As I got closer I could hear her say "Deep calls to deep," over and over.

As much as I wanted to get Tom's body out of my apartment, I had to reach Gloria first. She was my very best friend; to some, a woman touched with Dementia, but to those of us who can see into the Beyond, the wisest.

*Water Man, I need you.*

I could see what the dark shape was now; it was Mark. He held a gun to her back as he urged her closer to the garden fountain inside our park. What a fool, needing a gun to push around an old lady. I stopped and leaned against the wall to catch my breath. No doubt Mark and Tom had been in the thieving business together.

# The Water Man

Winkers always find each other to scheme with. He must plan on framing me with Tom's death, although I guess you can't call it framing considering I'm guilty. But if he figured out that Gloria is more than the medical community thinks she is, he knows she can point the police in his direction.

"Deep calls to deep." Gloria was near shouting it. I pushed off from the wall and headed toward her. Thunder rumbled above us, and one cool drop landed on my eyelash as I came within fifty feet of Gloria and Mark.

When I blinked, the raindrop slid into my eye, and for the first time I could see into the Beyond without a passing spirit opening the door for me.

The Water Man's Night Lights were everywhere. They filled the sky like giant fireflies chiseled out of the prayers of the Water Man's people—more thunder rolled across the sky from the flapping of their wings. I shuddered and put my hand over my chest as my heart galloped a little too fast. I only saw the Night Lights when someone passed on.

Once again, my thoughts flickered to Tom. If I hadn't killed him, he might have discovered the Water Man and received a

Night Light to escort him to the next life.

My gaze shot to the large fountain where Mark and Gloria quickly approached. Children had been sculpted to look like they were playing in the water; a boy held up a small girl who reached above her head to catch a butterfly. The round base of it glowed—not with the spotlights that cast the children in artificial light, but the brightest blue I'd ever seen.

It was in this beautiful blue that Mark tried to drown Gloria. *No.* I won't allow it. I closed in on Mark and pulled on his collar when he thrust Gloria's head in the water, but he was too strong for me. Not stopping to think, I grabbed the gun he had holstered in his back pocket and shot his leg. Mark let go of her and cradled his wound, rocking back and forth. I pulled Gloria from the water; she came up gasping. I took Mark's gun and I thrust it in her hands, and as best as I could, I told her to, "Rrrrrr!"

She looked at me, grabbed my wrist and said, "Deep calls to deep." Then she pressed her cold hand to the side of my face and smiled before fleeing the park.

An arm wrapped around my chest as I tried to follow her. I pulled away, and almost succeeded, but I had too little strength left after this torn apart day. Mark shoved me into the fountain with his bloodied hands; pushed me far enough in to where I had nothing to grab hold of, my arms grappling through the surge of blue for a lifeline. He leaned wearily on the edge of the fountain—I could see the triumph in his face through the waves.

His voice came muffled and slow, "That's for Tom, old man!"

*Water Man!*

I could see Him then, when the black started to fade from the sky and my hands looked young again as I reached out. The stream from the fountain poured over me as I lay in the deep. Stars were his eyes, and overwhelming love was his presence. As the blue waves broke over me bringing to my eyes my life in iridescent snap shots, I saw the Water Man at my side in each one. When Toby's father—my own son—walked out of our lives. When I lost my sweet Ginny, there He was holding me when I didn't even know it.

When I strangled Tom to protect Gloria, He whispered, "I love you" into my ear. The greatest love calling to me camped in my deepest, darkest moments.

Oh, Water Man.

When we rose from the water, I could see everyone, not as their bodies displayed, but as their souls did. Mark had a small, unkindled flame; he simmered red as he clutched his leg and sank to the ground. Suspended from the back of his shirt, as silver as a moonlit cloud, hung Gloria's bracelet.

I caught a glimpse of my own body, lying broken and worn in the fountain. Strange how it looked like a cast off shell.

Gloria shone like diamonds—almost as bright as a Night Light as she stood at the front desk, looking up at me. The college kid looked at her as if she was crazy, but I knew better. She hummed a song to me as we went along, me and the Water Man. No—Jesus. Oh how it feels good to have that word back again. We made one more stop before entering the Great Beyond.

Toby lay asleep in bed with his wife curled next to him. With the parting wisdom from Gloria, and my words fully restored, I spoke a legacy onto his wrist: the only thing I had to leave him; the words that will guide him through the deep parts. Jesus sealed the promise into his skin in black script: Deep calls to deep.

End

**Sherry Rossman** is the author of the bestselling Christian YA fantasy novel, *Faith Seekers,* as well as *Wake,* the first in the dystopian City of Light Series.

The Relevant Christian Magazine and Wordsmith Journal Magazine have published her recent short stories. Stepping into a new adventure, Sherry has become the leader of the newly formed Roots Writers Social Media & Critique Group, a project of Cataclysm Missions International.

She lives in Northern Arizona with her husband and children.

**Graxin**
By Kerry Nietz

Processing, always processing. Scanning the area before the pilot. Searching the terrain. Finding the indicators. Gathering data. Coalescing. Matrixing. Deciding. Marking or discarding. Perpetually at work.

There is *some* variability, though. On occasion, for instance, he likes to hum.

To an observer, XV-43 would appear unremarkable. A four-meter cube-shaped servbot with a triangle cage before it—its debris-clearing pilot—and rolling treads beneath.

Within the cube, protected, tucked neatly away, are the sensing devices. His measurement tools. Brought out only when needed. Atop the cube, as much for human familiarity as for function, is a circular head, colored gray. On it are red painted lips and white-painted teeth. Always smiling—clown-like—a face of designer whimsy.

His eyes are completely functional, though. They assist the other devices. They observe things as human eyes would: in color and in three dimensions.

# Graxin

Around him in all directions lies the surface of Proteus, Neptune's second largest moon. Or "Pro," as it is often called.

"Humans are ever shortening and simplifying," XV says to no one.

"Reducing the effort. Even with words. Stripping it down." It is a random observation. A diversion.

Like humming.

Proteus is a barren world. Not unlike Earth's own satellite. From horizon to horizon, it presents a darkened mass of craters, ridges, and valleys. Yet it has much to offer. And so, XV looks. Samples.

His decision matrix shifts. Like silt in an hourglass, the granules of thought begin to spin, compress, and flow in the same direction. They mound on the floor of his cranium. He stops. Extends a sampling device. Scoops into the grey, porous surface. Digs deeper and deeper. The arm retracts, folds neatly into his body. The testing devices stew on it, crush it, spread it, liquidate and oxygenate.

Finally, a decision is reached.

He has found more graxin.

A thrill runs through him and he signals his home. A few seconds later there is a response. An affirmation of his signal and his discovery. The harvesters are on their way.

XV-43 remains still for a moment. Allows his visual sensors to rise to the guiding planet above. Massive, blue, subtle bands, large spots of intense darkness. *Storms*, he's been told. Altogether majestic sight. Heavy. Looming. Yet still silent and waiting. Luminescent.

He looks to the horizon again. He occupies one of the darkest places in the solar system. A moon that fails to reflect the light sent it. A mere *taker* by galactic standards.

He cannot form a frown, but he has a semblance of the feeling. An echo of human emotion. He settles for merely shaking his head from side to side. Then he restarts his journey.

Processing, always processing.

Hours go by. He doesn't think in terms of days, because those have no meaning here. Proteus keeps one face always toward its parent, Neptune, so it rotates precisely as fast as it revolves. Convenient. Simple.

# Graxin

The sun and its ways are a distant memory. Barely brighter than the stars that make up the heavens around it. Insignificant. XV rarely thinks about the sun.

Only when a ship comes from that distant blue dot. But rarely do those come. Nor does he want them to. Ships bring complication. An unwanted distraction.

He begins humming again. A song his human instructor once taught him. About a dog and a window. He knows what the nouns in the song mean, of course. He knows what a *dog* is, a *window*, and *scraggily hair*. It is a silly song.

There is something more to it, though. A hint of longing for something visible but unattainable. XV wonders if longing is an emotion he was given. He feels it is. But he isn't certain.

He moves on, humming. Searching. Deciding. Scanning. And in his own way, enjoying the scenery. The dark barrenness of it. Mostly stone, with other base materials mixed in, base elements. Particulate hitchhikers from the world above. Only occasionally does XV encounter the compound used for human experiments in gravitation. Graxin.

XV glances to the heavens again. Studies the full blueness of the planet. Looming, but comfortable. Hanging overhead. Always overhead. Always watching.

An anomaly is detected. He turns to investigate. Fifty meters, forty meters, thirty meters…treads spin, wheels operate in near silence. Finally, he reaches the spot. He extends a sensor, touches the ground. Brings in a sample. Tastes it. Analyzes.

Another shake of his head. No graxin here. Only elemental jetsam in the sample. Rock and stone. Traces of ether, sulphur… but no graxin.

So why did he notice? What brought him here?

He scans the surroundings with normal vision. To the right and behind him, a high ridge begins. It circles in an almost uniform manner in front of him until it breaks sharply forward. There is a similar ridgeline to the left, he notices. High and sloped enough to make it difficult to see from overhead.

Curious. Such symmetry is rarely observed in nature. He checks his optics. Recalibrates. Dispels binocular vision and then restores it.

The pattern remains. It is like the

subtle entrance of a roadway. Only a fraction wider than he. Though cramped, he could explore it if he chose to.

XV scans the horizon again. Should he signal home? Ask for assistance?

There are only harvesters there. Automated takers and movers. Nothing of XV's caliber. Nothing like him. Technologically, he is alone.

He recalls lyrics from the song. About taking a trip, and leaving behind a sweetheart...

The decision is made. He moves forward. Slowly. Cautiously.

Humming.

He reaches the place where the ridgeline angles forward and begins to narrow. Here, the shadows are even darker, if it were possible. Proteus is the home of darkness. That doesn't concern him, though. He is a friend of darkness. What is a little less light? He has devices aplenty.

He hesitates for only an instant, then continues onward.

As he moves, he examines the walls of the ridge. There is variation to the surface. He can see this across the spectrum. From infrared to ultraviolet. Long furrows of lighter material. Wearing or tearing. His initial assessment says it is the result of volcanic forces, but other sensors beg to differ. They say water has played a part, either solid or liquid.

But that seems unlikely as well. The only water that has ever been found on Proteus is at the northern pole. And that is frozen and especially rare. Not enough to cause even the slightest change to its surroundings. Certainly, not enough to scratch a wall.

What else could affect the surface of Proteus, though?

He checks his service log. No harvester has ever been out this far.

The ridgelines meet overhead now, forming a natural arch. Curious. And wonderful! For the first time in thousands of hours, the planet Nep is completely hidden from his view. A verifiable change of scenery. Double darkness. It is like descending into a well, or a cavern.

Again, he thinks of the song. About reading. And robbers.

The "cavern" narrows even more. Tiny lasers touch the walls, assuring XV that he is all right. He won't get stuck. Won't be impeded in any way. The road is clear. Still wide enough.

# Graxin

Onward. Processing. Checking. Looking. Searching. His visible eyes hoping for something aside from darkness. His rational heuristics comfortable either way.

He detects a variation in the light level. Barely perceptible, but his sensors assure him it is there. A less dim darkness. A greying from black. He pauses for a moment, checks the walls on both sides, then moves forward again.

Proteus is a silent world, without atmosphere, but if it were not so, the sound his treads make would change from crunching to a soft whirring. The surface of the ground is different. He also detects a curve in the tunnel. Makes the proper adjustment.

Then brightness reigns. He dials back his visual sensors. Wishes for arms to shield his face. Turns his head regardless.

He has entered a place unexpected.

For here, there is light.

The walls of the chamber are shades of brown and gold, and there is a certifiable symmetry to the patterns. A framework of narrow arches that loop all the way around. The chamber is barely larger than XV himself. Five-point-seven meters, his instruments tell him. The ceiling above is just over half that distance.

In the exact center of the chamber is an object. A bump. A mound? It is perfectly symmetrical. In appearance, it is like four-meter-wide balls arranged in the form of a pyramid. So, from most angles, one ball atop two, though it is really one ball atop three.

They are all shining brilliantly. Spectacularly. Generating light out of the darkness.

Tentatively, XV extends his heat-sensing device, moves it carefully toward the object. It registers no temperature change whatsoever. The mound is generating light, but no heat. Remarkable.

He performs a battery of tests: spectral analysis, air sample, wind speed. Nothing unusual. The chamber might as well be out on the surface. It is all normal. Proteus normal.

Except it isn't. Not at all.

His presumption of volcanic action is dismissed. As is the effect of hydraulics or pneumatics. Neither fire, nor water, nor air formed this place. Arranged the pyramid of shining balls.

Then what?

He contemplates the harvesters. They are the only creatures on the moon that can transport substance, aside from him. They have limited intelligence, however. They would see no reason to make such a place. They would allocate no time for such an endeavor. They have one solitary purpose: harvest the graxin he finds. Contain it, strip it, grind it, and extract it. That is what harvesters do. Quickly and efficiently. Like metal locusts.

So, what causes this? Why is it here?

XV shakes his head. He has no idea. No human has ever been here. Aerial surveys were done. Graxin was found. He was deployed. Thousands of hours ago.

He thinks of planet Nep. That world is a sea of chilled gas. Crushing forces. Hydrogen, helium and "ices" such as methane and ammonia. Not the most adverse place in the solar system, but very nearly so.

Yet this chamber exists. Here.

It is wonderful. Surprising. Unusual.

And constructed. Has to be.

Hidden. Out of sight.

His song speaks of flashlights. Shining!

This is all outside his experience. Beyond his programming. No rules govern this. There aren't even suggestions.

XV swivels his head to look at the tunnel behind him. He should go. Return to his perpetual mission. Processing. Sampling. Searching. Leave this place for whatever specter had built it.

He looks at the mound again. Does it have a purpose? Did it ever?

He can make no guesses. He doesn't have the context to guess. To theorize. Not about this. It is wonderful, though. A welcome diversion. An anomaly.

His chronometer chimes. He has been in this chamber too long. Over an hour. Made no contact to the home, to the harvesters that wait. They will worry. Come to find him.

He reverses his motivator. Starts to back up the hall. Eyes fixed on the chamber of light. The brilliance of it. Rainbows seem to dance.

A question stops him. He draws carefully back into the chamber. What brought him here? Bots know nothing of chance. Of destiny.

Only one reason could be possible. Reluctantly, XV extends his most important sensor. Digs deeply into the floor of the chamber. Samples. Retracts the sensor slowly. Almost reverentially. Pulverizes the sample, sifts it...tastes it.

His motivator quickens. The chamber floor is nearly 90 percent graxin. He suspects the same could be said of the entire chamber. Those arches...the color is right. It is a veritable hoard. A lifetime of searching, combined into a single six-meter area.

His decision matrix shifts. Thought granules move, churn, spin, and plateau.

What should he do? The normal pathway is short. Simple. Signal home, bring the locusts.

His ever-smiling face pivots, turns, examines the chamber both up and down. Then he looks to the ground. Shakes his head.

Postponement. He is allowed that. Decisions can be belayed. Especially when safety is a concern.

The harvesters will wonder about *his* safety.

He retreats. Makes his way out.

Hurrying.

XV reaches the place where the ridge above begins to separate and feels the blue-green glow of Nep overhead. Specifically, he notices the curl of the planet's Great Dark Spot. A storm that has been raging for millennia. A storm that is constant. Consistent. Violent.

He scans the horizon around him. Notes the grey and slate palette. Also, consistent. Constant. Placid.

Yet he finds that his system is galvanized. His fluid flow rate is excessive given the situation. He authorizes correction routines, then runs a system diagnostic. Demands a slowdown. He still finds himself searching the surroundings. Digitally nervous.

There is no one here. Nothing to fear.

He redirects his thoughts. Forces his mind through familiar channels. Processing. Scanning. Always looking for more. Completing his mission. Finding graxin.

Humming. He needs to hum.

No bunnies, no kittens, no parrots.

The melody helps, but it doesn't restore his processes. Not completely. Something new has entered the matrix. Something he'll have to deal with.

# Graxin

No!

He deliberately moves ahead. Recalls normality. All he need do is find more graxin. Call the harvesters again.

He urges his treads to speed. Yes. He will find more graxin.

But not here. Nowhere close to here.

An hour later, XV locates the substance beneath a large and solitary outcropping of stone. His systems immediately relax. His decision matrix is satisfied. Temporarily.

He makes the call to the harvesters, but this time he waits for their arrival.

They bounce in on what appears to him to be legs made of nothing. Veritable whips beneath their shining round bodies.

With only a passing acknowledgement of his presence, they begin to burrow and dance. First five harvesters arrive, and then a dozen. They circle the area, picking it clean of all the precious material they can find. Moving like silver piranhas amidst a sea of charcoal. Little furrows in the sand. Digging and consuming, leaping into the sky before they reach another location.

Tenacious grazing.

They have graxin sensors of their own, of course. Short-range sensors.

Nothing as sophisticated as those in XV's array of instruments.

Thankfully.

XV shakes his head. Checks the blue-green planet again. He gets a power low reminder then. It is time for him to return home.

He watches as the harvesters reach the end of their task. Begin bouncing and skipping away toward the horizon. He follows them. Slowly. Every sensor turned inward to conserve.

Two hours later he reaches the white silo he calls home. Noting his arrival, the curved door slides aside, allowing him entry. It has an external manual lock. He has no idea why. It is vestigial. Another leftover mystery. Human mystery.

XV turns, reverses himself into the entrance. Aligns himself over the sunken charging station. He then feels the pressure of the cable as it ascends from beneath. The prick as the spigot attaches to his undercarriage. Feels the energy begin to flow. A burning wholeness.

Home is as utilitarian within as it appears from without. Only the necessary equipment amidst a room of antiseptic white. White walls, with grey mechanical arms on each side to break up the monotony. The required repair and refueling equipment. Little else.

White ceiling.

While he waits, XV attempts to tabulate his finds of the day. His successes. He cannot exclude the chamber, however. Can't block it out.

What makes it important? Special? Why is it any different than the kilometers of gravel and dirt he travels every day?

He does not know, but it is special. And not because of the large quantity of graxin.

Light in the darkness. Something that should not be. Something unusual.

It includes a large amount of the substance he seeks. It *should* be completely harvested. It is why he is here. On Proteus.

The decision matrix stalls. Flips twice. Granules move in the opposite direction.

He can't make that call. Can't harvest it.

So, should he just ignore it? Act as if the chamber was never found?

Yes. That is what he'll do.

XV deactivates his visual sensors—his eyes—and puts himself on half power. Now he will rest.

The decision is made.

Except the decision is *not* made. The very next day, XV finds himself again at the chamber. He searched for hours trying to avoid it, yet here he is, inside. Again.

Directly before him is the mound. The light is not constant, he realizes. Aside from the rainbows, there is a slight fluctuation in the light source. A feeling of life. Of permanence.

More curious now, he brings additional sensors to bear. He reaches out and samples the walls. He is surprised to find the remnants of a color additive laid atop the wall's surface. Designs had been painted there. He examines their structure across the spectrum. Yes, there are telltale coloring changes. A pattern. Drawings of bipeds. It might even be a story.

He references the few human records

he has. Trying to find a starting point, a similarity between what was and what he sees. But sadly, he has very little to work with. Luxuries like history, philosophy, and theology aren't necessary for a sampling bot. Especially one so far from the blue dot. Way out here.

His systems grieve for his lack. His disability. His creators gave him the capacity to hum and wonder—along with a painted smile—but nothing of real value. Nothing of depth. Only a task. An existence wholly defined by what he does.

He searches the room again. Wishes for the ability to really smile.

He has *this* now, though. A special place.

He nods. Yes. He has *this*.

Hundreds of hours go by. Hours of graxin searching mingled with visits to the chamber. No longer does he try to measure or probe its mysteries. All he does is sit and marvel. Delight in the colors. In the shimmering light.

Irreducible glory.

He derives theories as to its origin. To

its purpose. That perhaps Proteus once was populated, or that it was visited by extra-solar people. Travelers.

It is a captured moon, he knows. One that could have come from farther out. Out where the ice dwarfs live. Perhaps beyond Pluto and Eris and Haumea. Out where no probe or bot has ever been. No eye has ever seen.

Or maybe, just maybe, the chamber was formed with the moon. Made especially for him…

It is wild speculation. Yet he revels in it anyway. It makes the rest of his chores seem easier. Less mundane.

But still trivial in comparison.

It is during his most speculative and fulfilling visit that he ignores his chronometer. Forgets the time. Loses his place. Loses track.

And things change.

He exits the tunnel, backing out as he always does. He isn't two meters from the exit before his rear sensors detect something. Movement. A tingle of energy, nervousness, travels his pathways. He pivots and swings his body around. Aims the triangle pilot away from the entrance.

And he sees it.

Sitting completely still on the ground. Watching. Whip-like legs totally at rest, hanging like strands of hair from its side.

A single harvester. Shiny, silver, lone aperture for an eye. Nothing but blackness beyond that. Behind it. And it watches XV, having just exited the tunnel.

At first XV thinks the harvester is incapacitated, it remains so still. But the use of a radiation sensor tells him the harvester is functioning. It is alive.

Perhaps it is damaged? He sends a message to the silver spider, asking for its ident. After a short pause, it answers. The parity checks are correct. The harvester is fine. Only temporarily immobile. Voluntarily watching.

XV asks an important question: "Why are you here?"

The harvester studies him.

XV can feel the tickle of its rudimentary sensors in action. Probing him. Looking for anomalies.

Finally, the probing stops. "Your extended absence was detected. I was sent to find you. Determine if you need assistance. Do you?"

"I do not," XV messages back. "I am fully operational. Here's my latest system diagnostic and comparative baseline spec." He sends the data along. Waits.

Finally, the harvester moves. Sits up on its arms. Straightens. It then turns slightly, as if peering behind XV. "Were you encumbered?" Meaning "delayed due to situational circumstances."

XV bows his head. "I was. A narrow passage. Requiring slow movement."

"Is this place useful for harvesting? Should others come?"

XV feels the granules of his matrix begin to flutter and take flight. They spin around his cranium like a small sandstorm. Choking his reaction. Clogging the pathways. How should he answer?

"No fish!" says the song. Fish don't walk.

He shakes his head slowly.

With a slight nod, the harvester turns and bounces away.

XV pauses for a long moment. Scans the dark horizon, and then the giant overhead. He must return to work.

He can't ignore the disjointed thoughts that interfere. The fact that he doesn't want to leave.

Concern fills him. Worry that his chamber has now been discovered. What if the harvester doesn't believe him? What if some anomaly showed up in its scans?

What if it returns with the rest? The swirling, burrowing, unthinking rest.

The chamber would be destroyed. Completely.

He reassesses his thought processes. Bids the granules to slow, settle.

The harvester suspected nothing. It won't be back. XV will move on.

He waits another five minutes, just to be certain. Checks the surroundings again with all available sensors. Detects nothing. No motion whatsoever.

He resumes his work.

For hundreds of hours he avoids the chamber completely. He never waits for the harvesters to do their work. He simply calls them and moves on to the next find.

He even returns home for another charge. Yet while he is recharging, he is certain he hears the harvesters in the building plotting. Asking questions behind his back. Wondering about the exquisite find he is withholding. Hoarding. Questioning his sanity. His purpose.

Finally, he is certain what he must do. He'll never beat the harvesters in raw speed. They are too agile, too quick. So after his charge is complete, he leaves the white silo behind. He travels the now familiar path all the way to the place where the parallel ridges begin to converge. He doesn't bother to enter the chamber again. He knows what that will bring. The time it will require.

Instead, he turns and backs himself in as tight as possible. Fills the chamber's entrance with his bulk.

Then he waits.

Eventually, they come.

There are ten of them this time. They travel in the normal way, skipping and bouncing. There is no indication that this time is any different. No reverence for where they now are. They simply form a semi-circle two meters before him. And stop. Look at him.

"Why are you at this location again?" one of them messages.

XV holds his place. "I prefer it."

This brings more silence.

"Prefer?" The group turns toward each other. "No failures are sensed in this model. Yet its messages make no sense."

"We message over the same frequency," XV says, reminding them that he is present.

The harvesters appraise him again. "Tell us your purpose here. Is there graxin?"

XV readies his sensing devices. Steels himself. "It doesn't matter," he messages back.

The harvesters stall for a moment. "Doesn't matter? That is an inconsistent answer."

One harvester breaks free from the group. It begins slowly walking, like a silver daddy longlegs, to the perimeter of the clearing. It turns toward the ground, sniffing, scanning. It then stops and begins to bounce. "Graxin detected!"

The others leave formation and begin to circle the area. They get more agitated as they move. Some begin to harvest right there, others merely circle, as if unsure where to start. One—with the call letters HV-21—follows the ground unceasingly until it collides with XV's triangular pilot. His pushing structure. "The readings get stronger this way," it says. "There must be more. Behind." It appraises XV with its single black eye. "Please reposition, XV."

He shakes his ever-smiling head. "I will not."

The harvesters cease their churning. They quickly regroup in front of him. Close up. "You must move," they say in unison. "We cannot perform our task."

He shakes his head. "I will not."

The harvesters break into a frenzy, circling like ants caught in a thunderstorm. "You must," they repeat over and over, messages buzzing like mosquitoes in his receptors. "You must!"

But he does not.

Then the harvesters begin to leap. Trying to go over him. Around him.

He extends all his sensors. Engages everything that can do damage. Anything that has weight or heat. He moves and swivels. Pushes.

Arms sprawl. The battle is joined.

XV begins to hum.

# Graxin

Love needs something to protect. Scare away the dark.

It is six thousand hours before the ship from the blue dot arrives. The human passengers find XV parked alone within the silo. Home. His systems are in hibernate mode, the proper disposition for a bot in the process of charging.

Solstice, the younger of the two astronauts, walks to one of the interior walls and begins checking gauges. "There's a fair amount of graxin here," he says, squinting through his suit visor. "Can't seem to find any of the harvesters, though. There should be harvesters around, right? Cloistered above?"

Longstring, ever the weathered commander, shakes his head. "Probably out on a find." He indicates the sleeping XV. "These things keep them busy. Always searching. Sniffing it out." He nods toward a mounted screen. "Check the local stream."

XV awakens from his sleep. Moves smoothly forward.

The astronauts both pause, watching

as he moves toward the open door.

"See there," Longstring says finally. "Busy."

Solstice shrugs and sidesteps left. Peers closely at the screen. "No idents whatsoever." A puzzled look. "What does that mean?"

XV exits the silo, waits outside. The door begins to close.

Longstring joins Solstice at the gauges. Shakes his head. "It means we should go and look. We'll need to get some long-range scanning equipment. Have to be thorough."

XV begins to hum.

How much is that doggie in the window?

"Fine with me," Solstice says. "A little excitement. Up for some exploring when we're through? They say Proteus is one of the darkest places in the system. A captured moon. Never know what you may find…"

The silo door closes completely. XV unfolds a sensor arm. Uses it to manipulate the external manual lock. He then turns, begins his journey.

Processing, always processing. Finding the indicators. Gathering data. Deciding.

# Graxin

Marking or discarding. Perpetually at work.
Performing his mission. His *new* mission.
Behind him, he hears pounding on the
door. Calls to return. To set them free.

Limited time. Limited air!

His painted face only looks ahead.
Toward his chamber. His purpose.

Humans would only strip it down.

## End

**Kerry Nietz** is a refugee of the software
industry. He spent more than a decade of
his life flipping bits, first as one of the
principal developers of the database
product FoxPro for the now mythical Fox
Software, and then as one of Bill Gates's
minions at Microsoft. He is a husband, a
father, a technophile and a movie buff. He
is the author of several award-winning
novels, including *A Star Curiously Singing*,
*Freeheads*, and *Amish Vampires in Space*.

## THE BEAR ESSENTIALS:
—Short Tales
—Powerful Stories
—Good Price
—No Extra Frills

Bear Publications produces original short story anthologies from the universe of speculative fiction, including science fiction, fantasy, and horror. Many tales reverberate with Christian themes, but not all do.

Some are wrapped around a single original story world, like *Medieval Mars,* while others explore a common set of characters, like *Avatars of Web Surfer,* while yet others present stories without boundaries. See more at:

**www.bearpublications.com**

BEAR PUBLICATIONS

*Nothing but powerful short tales*